D1470233

Y
MCI

McIntosh, Kenneth,
    1959-

If the shoe fits.

$9.95   Grades 7-9

	DATE	

Schmaling Memorial
Public Library
Fulton, Illinois

AP 0 0 '10

DISCARD

BAKER & TAYLOR

THE CRIME SCENE CLUB: FACT AND FICTION

Devil's Canyon: Forensic Geography

Over the Edge: Forensic Accident Reconstruction

The Trickster's Image: Forensic Art

Poison and Peril: Forensic Toxicology

Close-Up: Forensic Photography

Face from the Past: Skull Reconstruction

The Monsoon Murder: Forensic Meteorology

If the Shoe Fits: Footwear Analysis

The Earth Cries Out: Forensic Chemistry and Environmental Science

Things Fall Apart: Forensic Engineering

Numbering the Crime: Forensic Mathematics

A Stranger's Voice: Forensic Speech

IF THE SHOE FITS

Footwear Analysis

Kenneth McIntosh

Mason Crest Publishers

IF THE SHOE FITS: FOOTWEAR ANALYSIS

Copyright © 2009 by Mason Crest Publishers. All rights reserved. No part of this publication may be reproduced or transmitted in any form or by any means, electronic or mechanical, including photo-copying, recording, taping, or any information storage and retrieval system, without permission from the publisher.

MASON CREST PUBLISHERS INC.
370 Reed Road
Broomall, Pennsylvania 19008
(866)MCP-BOOK (toll free)
www.masoncrest.com

First Printing

9 8 7 6 5 4 3 2 1

ISBN 978-1-4222-0259-3 (series)
Library of Congress Cataloging-in-Publication Data

McIntosh, Kenneth, 1959–
  If the shoe fits : footwear analysis / by Kenneth McIntosh.
      p. cm. — (The Crime Scene Club ; case #8)
  Includes bibliographical references.
  ISBN 978-1-4222-0253-1   ISBN 978-1-4222-1456-5
  [1. Criminal investigation—Fiction. 2. Forensic sciences—Fiction. 3. Mystery and detective stories.] I. Title.
  PZ7.M1858If 2009
  [Fic]—dc22
                              2008033243

Design by MK Bassett-Harvey.
Produced by Harding House Publishing Service, Inc.
www.hardinghousepages.com
Cover design by MK Bassett-Harvey.
Cover and interior illustrations by Justin Miller.
Printed in Malaysia.

CONTENTS

Introduction   7

1 De-Feeting Crime   12

2 Prisoner #37928   22

3 There Are No Guilty Prisoners   31

4 Prints from the Past   37

5 Sorting Out the Facts   47

6 Following the Truth   64

7 The Shoe Fits   72

8 The Exhibition   81

9 Halloween   96

Forensic Notes   103

Further Reading   139

For More Information   140

Bibliography   141

Index   142

Picture Credits   143

Biographies   143

INTRODUCTION

The sound of breaking glass. A scream. A shot. Then . . . silence. Blood, fingerprints, a bullet, a skull, fire debris, a hair, shoeprints—enter the wonderful world of forensic science. A world of searching to find clues, collecting that which others cannot see, testing to find answers to seemingly impossible questions, and testifying to juries so that justice will be served. A world where curiosity, love of a puzzle, and gathering information are basic. The books in this series will take you to this world.

The CSI Effect

The TV show *CSI: Crime Scene Investigator* became so widely popular that *CSI: Miami* and *CSI: NY* followed. This forensic interest spilled over into *Bones* (anthropology); *Crossing Jordan* and *Dr. G* (medical examiners); *New Detectives* and *Forensic Files*, which cover all the forensic disciplines. Almost every modern detective story now involves forensic science. Many fiction books are written, some by forensic scientists such as Kathy Reichs (anthropology) and Ken Goddard (criminalistics and crime scene), as well as textbooks such as *Criminalistics* by Richard Saferstein. Other crime fiction authors are Sir Arthur Conan Doyle (Sherlock Holmes), Thomas Harris (*Red Dragon*), Agatha Christie (Hercule Poirot) and Ellis Peters, whose hero is a monk, Cadfael, an ex-Crusader who solves crimes. The list goes on and on—and I encourage you to read them all!

The spotlight on forensic science has had good *and* bad effects, however. Because the books and TV shows are so enjoyable, the limits of science have been blurred to make the plots more interesting. Often when students are intrigued by the TV shows and want to learn more, they have a rude awakening. The crime scene investigators on TV do the work of many professionals, including police officers, medical examiners, forensic laboratory scientists, anthropologists, and entomologists, to mention just a few. And all this in addition to processing crime scenes! Fictional instruments give test results at warp speed, and crimes are solved in forty-two minutes. Because of the overwhelming popularity of these shows, juries now expect forensic evidence in every case.

The books in this series will take you to both old and new forensic sciences, perhaps tweaking your interest in a career. If so, take courses in chemistry, biology, math, English, public speaking, and drama. Get a summer job in a forensic laboratory, courthouse, law enforcement agency, or an archeological dig. Seek internships and summer jobs (even unpaid). Skills in microscopy, instrumentation, and logical thinking will help you. Curiosity is a definite plus. You must read and understand procedures; take good notes; calculate answers; and prepare solutions. Public speaking and/or drama courses will make you a better speaker and a better expert witness. The ability to write clear, understandable reports aimed at nonscientists is a must. Salaries vary across the country and from agency to agency. You will never get rich, but you will have a satisfying, interesting career.

So come with me into this wonderful world called forensic science. You will be intrigued and entertained. These books are awesome!

—Carla M. Noziglia MS, FAAFS

Jessa's Journal

Evening, October 1

Sometimes it feels like no one takes me seriously. Everyone listens to Maeve because she's so outrageous. And adults adore Lupe because "she's a real role model." They don't realize that she's so insecure she has to starve herself—literally—to stay thin.

I feel guilty writing this—but Lupe and Maeve probably write stuff about me in their journals, too. And I'm sick of being overlooked. I want to yell, "Hey, JUST BECAUSE I'M BLOND, THAT DOES NOT MEAN I'M A DITZ!

"How many blonds does it take to change a light bulb?"

Just one, if it's me. And I'll put in a compact fluorescent to help you save energy.

Maybe it's time to try dye? I'd hate to put chemicals in my hair. But maybe it's time for a new look?

No one listened to me when I was younger, either. Mom and I had gone to the doctor. The doctor sees I got a black eye and says, "What happened there, Jessa?"

The doctor must have thought Randy was one of my little friends. But he wasn't.

He was a real-life monster, scarier than any horror movie I've ever seen.

I still shiver, thinking back to the time that he lived with us. Mom and the Monster would sit on the couch smoking pot, drinking beer, and laughing at the TV, and I'd hide in my room wondering, "Where's my daddy and why doesn't he rescue me?" I always knew that sooner or later Mom would pass out, and then Randy would come looking for me.

Mom would pretend like she didn't know. But she did. A decade later, I still haven't forgiven her.

That day in the doctor's office, as we were leaving, the nurse stops us and asks, "Honey, who's Randy?"

I tell her, "Mama's boyfriend. He lives with us."

Mom puts on her sunshiny, smiley look and says, "Aren't children funny? She's imagining things." And then she turns to me and says, "Why, Jessa, honey, you hit your eye when you fell on the stairs."

Mom, why didn't you stand up to him? The shiner was the least thing he did to me. Did rent money mean more to you than I did?

Ten years later, we still don't talk about it.

Oh, well. Time for bed. School tomorrow, and CSC after. So that's something to look forward to. And Lupe and Maeve aren't really all that bad. They're my friends. Truth is, without the other kids in CSC, school—and life—would be a lot more boring.

Well, every day is a fresh beginning—so tomorrow could be a whole new start on something. Believing that beats going crazy.

I think.

Hey, I haven't gotten a letter from Lewis Henry lately. I wonder if he's all right.

Chapter 1
DE-FEETING CRIME

Jessa shouldered a large hemp bag containing her homework and accessories. "Everything but the kitchen sink" her mom always told her: make-up; perfume; calculator; keys to her home, school locker, and bicycle lock; paintbrushes and tubes of acrylic paint; a pitch pipe, a book of poetry, a little sketch pad, her iPod, and pepper spray. *Hey, it never hurts to be prepared.*

Closing her locker, she went outside, where the other students were leaving campus, getting in their cars, or walking to the bus stop. For most of her peers, the day at Flagstaff Charter School was over. But for Jessa and three other students, it was time for Crime Scene Club.

As she opened the door of the CSC lab, Jessa saw she was the last to arrive. Maeve sat in the front, her boots propped on a table, reading some awful fantasy novel with illustrated blood dripping all over the cover. Jessa believed strongly in each to their own, but Maeve would be a lot easier to relate to if she read Harry Potter or romances or mysteries or . . . anything not so dark and creepy.

Lupe was in the second row, smiling, chatting with the instructors. Jessa gave her a nod in greeting, and she waved in return.

Wire was in the back row. He was a total freaking genius, always plugged into some device. This afternoon, he was punching away at his laptop. He'd solved two cases the past year just by sitting and pressing keys. Social skills? Minimal. Brain density? Unbelievable.

"Hi, Jessa, have a good day?" Mr. Chesterton asked. He was their science teacher and the CSC school sponsor. If anyone had anything bad to say about Mr. C, it would be news to Jessa. He was like Santa Claus, only his beard was red instead of white, and he hung around all year long.

"Just fine, Mr. C." Jessa knew his question wasn't a real one; he didn't want to hear the truth.

Detective Kwan smiled at her. "Oh, Jessa, I have pictures from this summer's LA trip. I'll send you the files." Ms. Kwan was the Flagstaff Police Department's representative for the group. Jessa sometimes thought that Dorothy Kwan came into the world in order to provide some sort of karmic balance in her life for her own mother. While her mother lived life as loose and easy as she could, everything about Detective Kwan was neat, precise, and orderly. She had a brain like that character Spock on the ancient *Star Trek* show, and a wardrobe so slick and pressed down she could have stepped out of the window from one of those really expensive department stores. And to top off all that perfection: she really cared about students.

Schmaling Memorial
Public Library
Fulton, Illinois

When Jessa's art instructor died—murdered by her husband—Ms. Kwan had helped Jessa stay sane. Sometimes she thought Ms. Kwan was just too good to be true, like maybe she was merely a figment of her own imagination. But there she sat, in her little black suit and her shiny black hair, apparently as real as anyone else in the room. Just seeing her always made Jessa feel like the world might not be such a bad place after all.

"Today we're going to learn about one of the oldest crime solving techniques," Mr. Chesterton announced.

"Clubbing perps on the head?" Maeve always has to make a wisecrack.

"Footprint analysis," Detective Kwan said. "Every day, we hasten about our business and—never thinking about it—we leave tracks. It only takes a split second to step in a muddy spot or trail dirt onto a carpet, but the work of a moment can last—"

"An unbelievably long time," Mr. Chesterton finished.

Tag-team teaching. Jessa grinned. *They're starting to sound like an old married couple, finishing each other's sentences.*

"The first human-like creatures," Mr. C continued, "called *Australopithecus*, walked across an African mud flat more than three million years ago—leaving tracks that you can still view in a museum today."

"Famous and legendary figures have left their footprints for posterity as well," Detective Kwan added.

Where did she ever learn to talk like that? Why don't my words come out all smooth like hers do?

"For instance," the detective was saying, "you can see if your shoe size matches that of Jack Nicholson outside Grumman's Chinese theater, where the stars leave their marks. Or the three greatest religious leaders of the world—Buddha, Mohammad, and Jesus—are all said to have left footprints. Not everyone believes they're authentic, but they're now displayed in various sacred shrines."

"But today," Mr. C said, "we're looking at a less legendary and more practical application for footprints—crime solving. Footprint analysis is a classic technique in crime cases. Fictional detective Sherlock Holmes, the famous Victorian sleuth, solved cases based on prints."

"Oddly," Detective Kwan continued, "footprint evidence is often overlooked in the twenty-first century. Other forms of evidence—DNA analysis, fingerprinting, and so on—are more often at the forefront of investigators' minds. At the same time, criminals—like their law enforcement counterparts—tend not to think about their feet. In recent years there have been cases where the perpetrators wore gloves to conceal their fingerprints and even hairnets so they wouldn't leave DNA traces—but they left unmistakable footprints, adequate to convict them."

"Well, that makes sense," Maeve interrupted. "Gloves are cool and so are caps—no one's really going to notice all that much if they see someone wearing gloves and some sort of hat. But wouldn't

it look funny to see someone wearing plastic boo-
ties over their shoes?"

"Good point," Detective Kwan agreed. "That's
one reason why so many perps leave footprints."

Lupe put up a hand.

"Yes?"

"Isn't there a big difference between footprints—
and fingerprints or DNA? I mean, I wouldn't think
that footprints would be as credible when it comes
to convicting someone. After all, your fingerprint
or DNA signatures are totally unique. There are bil-
lions of people, but no one else shares my fingerprint. On the other hand, if Maeve and I go to the
mall and buy the same kind of shoes—"

"I would *never* buy prissy shoes like yours,"
Maeve interjected.

"I'm just saying what if." Lupe made a face at
Maeve. "Then if one of us—let's say Maeve—committed a crime, and they got her shoeprints, they
might grab me and think I'm the criminal."

"Hey! How come I do the crime? You're stereotyping me," Maeve protested.

"I think we understand Lupe's point," Mr. Chesterton said. "And she's right. Footprint evidence is
not necessarily unique."

"Entirely correct." Ms. Kwan smiled at Lupe.
"That's why criminals are rarely convicted solely on
the basis of footprints. Footprints can point investigators in the right direction—but shoe marks are
rarely case closers."

"Unless there's something unique about the
shoe." Wire's voice was a monotone, and he didn't

even raise his head from staring at the monitor of his computer.

How does he do that? He's probably in the middle of an online role playing game—and still following this discussion, too.

Wire continued in his flat voice, his fingers still flying over the keyboard. "As soon as the two of you buy those pairs of identical shoes, you'll begin to alter them. Like Lupe's dad owns an auto paint business, and she helps him at work—so she'll have traces of paint on those shoes. And Maeve's home is out in the woods—so she'll have dirt in the cracks. And then you two probably walk differently. Let's say Lupe wears out the heel of her shoes and Maeve wears out the middle of the soles. After six months wearing those shoes, each pair will leave an entirely distinct mark."

"Yeah, but you'd need perfect prints to see those differences," Lupe argued. "Most footprint evidence isn't that perfect."

It's the battle of the brains: Nancy Drew versus Technical Support.

"Great discussion." Mr. C looked thoughtful. "I think this begs for an experiment."

"Okay then." Ms. Kwan set a briefcase on the lectern in front of her and snapped it open. "Wire, since you began this discussion, would you be so kind as to go out back of the lab and run back and forth for a few moments?"

"No way. It's muddy back there. These are new shoes. Besides, I have to keep dirt out of my trailer or it'll mess up my hard drives."

"I'll go." Maeve jumped up and ran out the door.

Ms. Kwan pulled an object out of her case. "Now we need a volunteer to take prints."

My turn. Jessa put her hand up.

"Great." Ms. Kwan handed her a cardboard box. "Jessa, go out back of the lab—be careful not to step on any of Maeve's prints—then open up this container and press the casting material as hard as you can into the print. Wait a few moments, and then bring it back in the room."

After Maeve and Jessa returned, Detective Kwan showed the club how to change the cast from Maeve's boots into a negative image cast, using fixative and a foam molding kit. Half an hour later, Ms. Kwan called the club back to order and asked, "Maeve, would you mind removing your right boot for a moment?"

"Well, I need to warn you, I didn't get a shower this morning. . . ."

"I think we can deal with it."

"Okay. Hold your noses." She pulled off her boot and handed it to the detective.

Ms. Kwan pointed to the sole. "Notice the indentations here and here. It looks like nails or something hard got stuck and then fell out? You can also see that the heel is worn on this side," she pointed, "but not this other side. Clearly, this boot is rather unique." Detective Kwan pressed the shoe into the molded form. "And voila—the shoe fits."

"Lame." Wire pronounced.

"Pardon?" Mr. C responded.

"If Maeve were planning some awful crime in this building, she'd walk on the sidewalk, not in the

mud, so you wouldn't have that lovely cast or any other kind of footprint."

Detective Kwan smiled. "So, in your hypothetical situation, Maeve is going to commit some heinous deed right here, in this room?"

"Yep."

"All right. And we'll assume she's wiped any dirt off her feet so as not to leave any prints on the carpet."

"Of course I'd wipe my feet," Maeve agreed.

"Okay. So Maeve, go back to the door, then walk in and come up in front of me, where you're going to commit some crime."

Maeve shook her black hair out of her eyes and complied.

"Thank you. Step aside a moment, please. Now, Jessa, would you be our CSI tech again?"

"Sure."

Detective Kwan reached inside her briefcase and pulled out a spray bottle filled with liquid. "This is leuco-crystal-violet. Very carefully, walk around Maeve's path, then spray this down on the carpet where she walked."

Jessa did so. As she squirted the liquid onto the carpet, dark purple prints suddenly appeared, one after another.

"Whoa." Even Wire was impressed.

Lupe leaned down to look closely. "Here's a lighter spot where it looks like there's a nick the sole. It's just like the cast."

"And you can tell the side of the heel was worn more because it's also a lighter mark," Ms. Kwan added.

"Our perpetrator has been de-feeted," Mr. Chesterton announced.

The club groaned.

"Just stick with science, Mr. C," Maeve begged him. "Don't try to be funny."

After the club was dismissed, as Jessa and Lupe were walking out together, Lupe asked, "Hey, have you gotten any letters from your prisoner pen-pal lately?"

Jessa frowned and shook her head. "Not for a while. I'm kind of worried about him."

"What's his name again?"

"Lewis Henry. I'm wondering what's going on with him."

But by later the same afternoon, Jessa didn't have to wonder any longer.

Chapter 2
PRISONER #37928

Jessa stopped by her locker and pulled on a thick, wooly sweater before biking home, then added a jean jacket over that, not caring if the layers made her look frumpy. She waved at the others: Maeve in her ancient, smoke-belching Volkswagen; Wire in his equally decrepit open-topped Jeep; and Lupe on her smart Italian motor scooter. *That's okay,* Jessa thought as she straddled her Schwinn three-speed, complete with fenders, lights, basket, and horn. *When the oceans rise and crops die, it won't be my fault.*

She pedaled down the gravel exit from Flagstaff Charter School onto the Fort Valley Road bicycle path. On her way, she passed several groups of students and waved at them, then stopped to chat with an older neighbor who was walking her dog. Once she reached the small, red-rock house she shared with her mother, she checked their mailbox. She found an envelope with the return address: State Penitentiary, Prisoner #37928

"You should try something I do—correspond with a prisoner," Sarah Crown had told her nearly a year ago, before her death. "It's a great thing to do when you're feeling depressed with your own life."

"You mean a criminal?" Jessa had been aghast at the very idea.

"Exactly."

"That's creepy. The prisoner will get out and—something bad will happen."

"Ah, Jessa. You need to have faith in the human soul."

"Maybe, but . . . not a male inmate. Men just . . . They're all out to do us in somehow." Remembering what she had said made Jessa wince now; her words had proved to be all too true in Sarah's life.

But Sarah had smiled with that calm look she used to wear so often. "Maybe you should rethink that viewpoint. Even the worst people have some good in them. It would be a risk for you—pushing outside of your comfort zone—but it could also be an eye opener for you."

Her art teacher's advice had eventually led to Jessa's correspondence with prisoner #37928, Lewis Henry—a man doing life for killing an FBI agent.

When she first got his name, Jessa did some Internet research and looked up the murder case. It was a standoff on the Navajo Nation between radical Native activists and the Diamondback Uranium Mining Corporation. The case was decided off the reservation because it involved a federal agent's death. Henry, a Navajo, was quickly tried by a white jury and convicted to life in prison.

After exchanging a few letters with Mr. Henry, Jessa was surprised to discover he was a sensitive, artistic soul. Lewis Henry, now past middle age, shared his fears, stunted hopes, and dashed dreams in his letters to her. Jessa now considered Lewis Henry to be a genuine friend, even though the two had never met face to face.

Inside her house, she dropped down on the faded couch and tore open the envelope. Lewis Henry's letter began with his usual Navajo word of greeting.

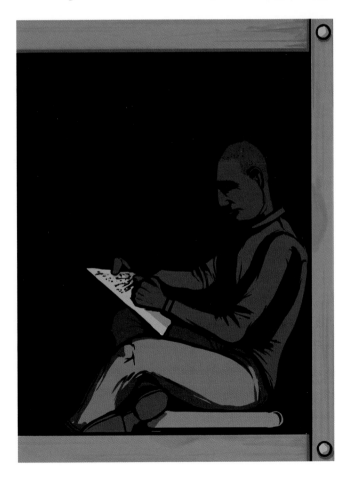

Yaateh, Jessa.

It is always good receiving your letters.
I can tell from your writing that you are
very intelligent—the way you put words
together is like poetry. If my life had
turned out different, I would have been
proud to have a young woman like you as
my daughter.

   I also received the painting you
sent, "Devil's Canyon at Sunset." They
removed the frame—can't have sharp,
wooden objects in here. (I might just
bust out of this super-max facility,
take a guard hostage and all that, all with
a picture frame. Hah!) Anyway, your
landscape piece is amazing. As you know,
I dabble with painting. As a reward for
a decade and a half of "good behavior,"
I'm allowed a brush and a few tubes
of paint. But your art is a whole lot
better than mine. That canyon isn't too
far from where I used to live, and your
painting of it looks so real—it sure brings
back memories. I can't thank you enough
for sending it.

   You asked about my life in here.
Sure you really want to know? Most
folks get freaked out by knowing about
it—but you've been writing me long
enough so I guess you really do want to
learn about it. So here goes.

The cells we live in are called "pods." There's no privacy—not even when you pee—because the guards are always looking at each pod through TV monitors.

Carlos and I live twenty-three hours, every day, in this little pod with its unpainted cement floor, wall, and ceiling. The pods were built for lone prisoners, but there isn't enough money for new prisons, so now we have to double up.

You probably imagine bars on the front of the cell, like in zoos or the old prison movies. Not nowadays. Instead, there's this steel wall with thousands of little holes in it. It allows the guards to see in, but there's no way to pass anything through the wall.

We prisoners can shout to each other, though. That's entertainment, every waking hour almost. That and TV. We shout back and forth about what's on TV—and the guys threaten each other, say bad words, tell jokes we've all heard a thousand times.

Believe me, this is no kind of life. The whole place smells bad, too, like a locker room mixed with a sewer. After all these years, I forget about it, though, at least most of the time. It's just when I come inside after being out in the exercise court that it hits me again.

For an hour each day, the guards allow just a few of us—the ones who can "play well together"—out into the exercise court to shoot hoops. That's the best part of the day. But it can also be scary. You never know who's in a good mood, and who's going to go crazy.

Like I said, the past few years they've allowed me to paint. Boy, is that a blessing. I paint horses, wildlife, and the mountains. It's been so long since I've seen these things, sometimes I wonder if I've got it right.

Besides painting, the other thing that keeps me sane is once-a-month visits from my spiritual adviser, Stanley Peshlaki. He's a haatali, a traditional healer. Used to be they just had the Christian chaplain here. The chaplain's a nice guy but I don't really relate to bilagaana religion. (That's the Diné word for white folk. Hope I'm not offending you. Don't know what you think about religion.)

Speaking of Stanley, he says he knows you! He said your club helped him when some guy made death threats against him last year.

Anyway, Peshlaki is a great guy. He makes the long drive down even though they don't pay him to come, and he tries to cheer me up. He sprinkles corn pollen and sings to purify the cell of bad spirits and curses. I'm sure glad. This place is nothing but evil and curses."

Medical care here is "minimal." I have diabetes that gets worse and worse. I keep telling them about my dietary needs and that we need to keep checking my blood, but they don't listen and that's kind of scary because I could die from it, and they know it. But honestly, maybe it is better this way. I don't want to live a real long time in here.

This is going to sound crazy, I know, but despite all the bad stuff I'm managing to live in hozhoni (that's the Diné word for "harmony.") Being stripped away from everything good in the material world allows the real self to grow strong—and in here, it is grow strong or go crazy. Before incarceration, I listened to my elders and learned about sacred ways, but that was just talk. Now it is real.

One other thing. You haven't asked about this, but I want to tell you. I swear by the spirits of my ancestors and by the four sacred mountains—I did not kill that FBI agent. I feel sorry for his family. I wish it had never happened, I wish they could have their husband or father back. It's an awful thing to lose someone like that. But I did not pull the trigger that killed him.

I wasn't exactly a brave warrior that day. The bullets started whizzing and banging off the rocks, and I just hid behind a big boulder. I could hear Victor and Dan up the hill behind me, banging away with their guns, and the FBI agent with the company man down the hill in front of me, shooting back at them. The FBI guy had an automatic weapon and that thing just kept going, "pap-pap-pap," filling the air with bullets. That's why I was hiding. Then I heard two shots right next to each other down the hill, a bit louder than the FBI guy's gun, and after that everything went silent. I waited, then got up from behind the boulder and walked down, real cautious like, to see what was happening.

I came around a ridge, where I assumed the two white guys were holed up, and I saw the federal agent, lying there, with a shot right through his head. I felt sick. If you haven't seen a thing like that, you can't believe how awful it is. You see a deer or elk that's been shot, and they're just meat and you don't think much about it. But to see a person—handsome young guy, too, lying there in this pool of blood—well, it's something you don't ever want to see again, believe me.

So I'm just standing there staring, trying not to lose my lunch on the ground, when the Diamondback guard comes around the other side of the ridge, looks at me, points his rifle at my chest and screams, "Don'tcha move, you murderin' Indian—I've gotcha now." The tribal police arrived, and well, the rest, as they say, is history.

You can believe me or not. I'm not asking for sympathy. I figure you write me assuming I'm a murderer and that shows how wonderful your compassion is. Bless you, Jessa. I'm just telling you because you're a very special person—and I want you to know I'm not the awful guy you probably think I am.

As the saying goes, "Keep those letters coming." You're my lifeline to the outside world.

Your friend,
Lewis Henry

Chapter 3
THERE ARE NO GUILTY PRISONERS

"Check it out! The dreads have changed color," Maeve whispered to Lupe as Jessa came into the CSC lab.

Shocks me, too, when I look in the mirror, Jessa admitted to herself.

"I like it," Lupe said. "What made you do it?"

Jessa shrugged. "I thought maybe red is more my color."

Wire squinted at her through his glasses. "Makes you look like Joss Stone, only your hair's all matted and you weigh more."

"Thanks, Wire, you're such a master of tact." But she knew the socially stunted genius didn't mean any harm, so she didn't really feel insulted.

Detective Kwan was looking at Jessa with her head cocked slightly to one side, like some glossy little bird. "It's very, ah . . . vibrant, Jessa," she said, obviously choosing her words carefully.

"I bet she just got tired of dumb blond jokes," Maeve said.

Jessa glared at her, but as usual, Maeve was saying whatever was on her mind. *Is it better to be tactful and careful all the time, like Detective Kwan, Jessa wondered, or blurt out what you really think, like Maeve? Or is it better to be somewhere in the middle?*

"Okay, let's get down to business." Detective Kwan sat on a stool in the front of the room. "So, CSC members, what do you want to learn about next?"

"We don't want another class," Maeve replied. "How about assigning us a case?"

The detective's mouth tightened. "I'm sorry, club, but you know I can't do that. You're just too much of a liability. I mean, that double murder last month wasn't even your case—this group wasn't supposed to have anything to do with it. And then Maeve was held at gunpoint and—"

"That's because I was set up by my sicko uncle," Maeve interrupted. "It wasn't the club's fault."

"But that was the sixth time in a year that you students have been endangered," the detective reminded them. "Sorry, but no more live cases."

Jessa slid her hand up.

"Yes?"

"How about a not-live case?"

"You mean a murder? We've had too many of those, Jessa."

"No, I mean, how about we investigate a closed case?"

"Uh, we'd do that because. . . ?"

"Because they got the wrong guy. There's a man in prison for life, and he's innocent."

Detective Kwan looked interested. "An innocence case? That could be a valuable experience for the club. Can you tell us more about the situation?"

"I correspond with this guy named Lewis Henry. He's incarcerated for allegedly killing an FBI agent a long time ago."

"I've heard of the Henry case, but I thought it was nailed shut. Why do you think he's innocent, Jessa?"

"He's really compassionate and artistic, and he told me in his last letter—"

Wire's deadpan voice interrupted, "There are no guilty prisoners. At least none who will admit it. According to my research, with very rare exceptions, inmates always protest their innocence. 'I was framed—it was this other guy.' Or, 'I'm a victim of prejudice.' They all have their story."

"But he's had a spiritual awakening," Jessa blurted.

"Right." Wire shook his head and went back to poking at his keyboard. "Every prisoner gets religion—even mass murderers—because it gains them a sympathetic audience."

"Wait a minute, Wire," Lupe said. "You saying people can't change? Because I know they can."

"Yeah, well, that works for you, but I see things scientifically. Prisoners go out of jail with the same combinations of DNA and hormones they went in with. That's why recidivism rates are so high, and that's why—"

"Hold on," the detective interrupted. "I've decided we'll go with Jessa's suggestion. This will be a good exercise for the club's crime-scene skills. I'll requisition everything on the case—transcripts, photographs, and as much of the hard evidence as they'll let out of the vaults. We'll go over the case with a fine-toothed comb, then discuss whether there's any merit to the prisoner's claim of innocence. We should have the files here by Monday. In the meantime, read up on the case. You'll find a number of old news articles on the Internet."

After Detective Kwan dismissed the club, she waited until the others left. Then, as Jessa gathered her things, she asked, "Jessa? What is this really about?"

Jessa met the detective's eyes. "Innocence. I don't think Lewis Henry is guilty."

"And?"

"And nothing. That's it."

"In my experience, there are usually personal reasons when I decide to go out on a limb for someone." Ms. Kwan smiled. "Think about it."

Jessa tried to return the detective's smile. "Thanks, Ms. Kwan. I will."

She didn't want to think about it. But she'd do most anything Ms. Kwan asked.

Jessa's Journal

CSC is going to reexamine Lewis's case. I should be glad, it was my big idea. But I'm conflicted about it.

"What is this really about?" Detective Kwan asked me. Good question. So I've been trying to find an answer. And here's what I've come up with: It's about the fact that someone has to stand up for the innocents in this world.

Why?

Because there was no one to stand up for little Jessa when she needed protection.

I still remember the cigarette smell of the plaid shirt Randy always wore, the way those huge rough hands felt on my skin. He always seemed like he was about a thousand times bigger than me.

And I remember the way Mom would look at me, all guilty, but never admitting it. She still looks at me like that.

Where is Randy now? I've been afraid to ask Mom, or even think about it. But I hope to God he's in jail somewhere—or dead. I know, it's awful to wish anyone dead, but it's more awful to think he's alive and free. If there's justice in this universe—if there is some great universal righter-of-wrong, then how can Randy not deserve to suffer? Not just for what he did to me either, because who knows who else he abused?

So anyway, I can't change my past, I can't do anythin to help little Jessa—but maybe I can make a difference now for someone else. No one believes Lewis Henry. N one is standing up for him. So I have to be the voice the voiceless, because I know what it feels like whe no one listens to you, when no one believes you.

Soon, we'll all learn the truth about the Diamondback shootout and the FBI agent's death. Maybe that's what scares me, though. What if Lewis is using me? Then he'd be just another m who's let me down, another guy who's trying to take advantage of me somehow, like all the re of them.

I pray to God (whoever She is): Please don let it be so.

Chapter 4
PRINTS FROM THE PAST

"Finding loopholes in all these documents will be like finding a needle in a haystack." Jessa frowned as she and the other CSC members surveyed the piles of folders and boxes that covered their lab's tabletops.

"The Lewis Henry case generated a great deal of public attention," Detective Kwan explained. "We have plenty of material to work through."

"So then," Mr. Chesterton said, "we'd better get started. What have you learned about the basics of the case?"

"The shooting happened on November 4, 1991, a Monday," Wire volunteered.

"It took place in Two Owls, on the Navajo Nation," Lupe added.

"The basic issue was the opening of the Diamondback Uranium mine," said Maeve.

"And what do you know about Diamondback?" asked Mr. C.

"They're an environmental disaster," Jessa replied. "They dig huge pits, completely spoiling the landscape, and there have been a pile of cases in which workers claimed exposure to harmful radiation. For the Native activists, opposing Diamondback was a religious obligation."

"To balance that perspective," Wire put in, "consider the fact that Diamondback provides badly needed jobs on the Navajo Nation. They've successfully countered all charges of negligence toward their workers. And nuclear fuel from their mines might be vital for a post-petroleum future."

Detective Kwan intervened. "You can debate the merits of uranium mining in earth science class. What matters now is to understand the motives of the principal actors on November 4, a decade and a half ago."

"It's like Jessa said," Lupe said. "The three Native activists belonged to a group called Act Now, and they were determined to stop Diamondback. They were armed and waiting for the company workers to try and force their way into the mine. Apparently the Act Now crew was willing to kill or be killed over this issue."

"They saw themselves like the T-shirt slogan," Maeve added. "You know—'Homeland Security: Fighting Terrorism Since 1492.'"

"Let's look closer at the two parties." Detective Kwan was clearly trying to get the club back on task. "What do we know about the individuals involved?"

Wire read from a court document in front of him. "'The three activists involved in the shootout were Lewis Henry, aged 39, Dan Twogoats, aged 27, and Victor Benally, aged 26.'"

"Wait a minute!" Jessa's pulse quickened. "That wouldn't be the Victor Benally who. . . ?"

Detective Kwan leaned over Wire's shoulder to see another document from the file. "Judging by this picture, I'd say almost certainly, he is—"

"Ken B's father," Maeve finished. "Would you believe a guy involved with a gang like this would grow up to be a straight-laced Flagstaff police officer?"

"Ken's dad was involved? This is creepy," Lupe said.

"I wouldn't use the word 'gang,'" Jessa corrected. "He was an environmental activist."

"A violent one," Wire countered.

"An important element in detective work," Dorothy Kwan reminded the club, "is remaining objective. Our beliefs about the parties involved are irrelevant. The only question is, 'Who shot whom on that day?'" She paused a moment. "It's also a good reminder that people come to law work from all manner of backgrounds."

Jessa heard what Ms. Kwan was saying, but she could no longer focus. What role did her ex-boyfriend's father play in this incident? Did Ken know what his father was doing in 1991? Jessa picked up a pencil and began doodling on her notebook. Why should she care, anyway? That relationship was dead. She just wished her feelings would die with it.

"What about the Diamondback side of the conflict?" Mr. Chesterton asked. "Who was involved on the other end of the gunfight?"

"The victim was a rookie FBI agent named Frederick Allen," Wire informed the club. "He was twenty-eight years old, and this was his first major case. The Diamondback company called the Feds in to see what they were up against, trying to establish their business on the Reservation."

"He left a widow and an unborn child," Lupe added. "Her name was Ella Allen."

"There was another man involved," Detective Kwan prompted, "who became chief witness in the investigation."

"Robert McClintock." Jessa managed to re-focus her thoughts on the case. "He was fifty-two, an armed guard for Diamondback Corporation."

"Look at the event as a military situation," Detective Kwan suggested. "How would you describe the encounter?"

"Pow-pow, bam-bam! Aagh!" Maeve answered.

"Very poetic, Maeve. Can someone be more precise?"

"There was a clearly defined strategic goal," Wire answered. "The FBI agent and company guard were attempting to unlock a chained gate, leading onto the Diamondback property. For several weeks, armed activists had camped in front of the gate, vowing to resist company employees."

Lupe took up the story. "Around eight that morning, Allen and McClintock pulled up in a company truck and walked uphill toward the gate. The activists were waiting, behind stone columns near the entrance to the property. They fired at the two men. The activists said they gave warning shots, but the men approaching didn't see it that way."

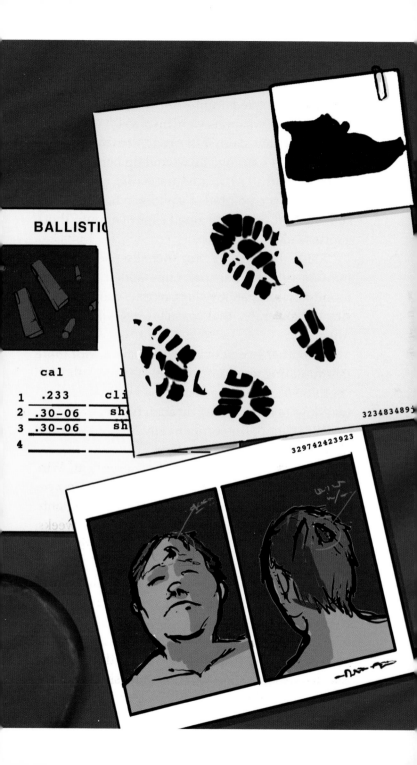

"You kids have really done your homework." Mr. Chesterton looked impressed. "Can you tell me what kinds of weapons were involved?"

"Yeah," Maeve said. "FBI Agent Allen was the best armed—so it's strange he wound up being the one killed. He had an AR15 automatic rifle, and according to this," she pointed at a paper in her hand, "he squeezed off three-and a half clips of ammo. That's a lotta lead."

"Ken's dad—uh, Victor Benally—held a .223 hunting rifle with scope," Lupe added. "I haven't found anything about slugs of that caliber at the site. At any rate, that wasn't what killed Agent Allen."

"The other two activists were armed with more incriminating weapons," Mr. Chesterton explained. "Both held .30-06 long arms. The victim died from two slugs of that caliber, through the head."

"What about the company guy, McClintock? Did he have a weapon?" Jessa asked.

The CSC members were quiet for a few minutes as they shuffled through the records, looking for the answer to the question. "Here's his own testimony," Lupe said finally. "He said he was firing in the activists' general direction with a rifle." She frowned. "That's pretty vague."

"It is," Ms. Kwan agreed. "What do we know about the shootout?"

Maeve shook her head, staring at pages in her hand. "Either everyone's a liar—or none of the combatants shot to kill. There were slugs all over the scene—flattened on boulders, stuck in the company truck, and in the fence behind the activists—but no one claims to have seriously targeted the opposing parties."

"But someone aimed carefully," Lupe said, "right at Agent Allen's forehead."

"Wrong," Wire said.

"Huh?"

"At the *back* of his head. Look at this picture."

"Oh, gross. . ."

"That's the back of his head, relatively clean holes, compared with this one," Wire said in his usual matter-of-fact voice.

"Yeesh!" Lupe looked sick

"Yeah." Maeve leaned to get a better look. "That's his forehead, splintered in pieces. Obviously exit wounds."

"Consistent with McClintock's testimony," Detective Kwan concluded. "He told the court," she read aloud from a print-out, "'I rounded the big boulder, and there was this guy (witness points at Lewis Henry, seated in the room) standing behind Frederick Allen's body, his gun still smoking.'" Detective Kwan added, "That word 'behind' fits the placement of the FBI agent's corpse and trajectory of the bullet."

"What about ballistics?" asked Wire. "Did the fatal slug match Henry's gun?"

"I've got that here." Maeve read aloud, "'Forensics expert Somers Blandish testified, "The slugs are badly damaged. The weight proves they came from a .30-06 long arm, but the rifling was too corrupted for a positive match.'"

Mr. Chesterton stroked his beard. "So the bullets were consistent with Lewis Henry's gun—or the gun that belonged to Dan Twogoats."

"But Twogoats was at least 150 feet away, and positioned *in front* of the agent," Wire countered. "*All* the witnesses agreed to that fact."

"Only two people could have shot Frederick Allen," Detective Kwan concluded. "Lewis Henry—or the company guard, Robert McClintock."

"And only one of those two—Lewis Henry—had a motive to shoot the agent," Lupe added. "McClintock and Allen were on the same side."

"So," Mr. Chesterton concluded, "it came down to two opposing statements. Henry claimed that he walked onto the scene and found the agent dead, but McClintock testified that the Navajo man was holding the smoking gun—literally."

"Jessa, I don't think this is looking very good for your pen pal," Maeve said.

But Jessa was lost in thought, staring back and forth between documents.

"What have you got there?" Detective Kwan asked.

"Maybe nothing, but. . ." Jessa held up a photograph. "This has a notation, 'Lewis Henry shoeprint.' It goes along with this little sketch." She pointed to another paper. "It shows the position of the Lewis Henry shoeprint in relation to the victim's body—and makes the point that the print's position goes along with the direction of the fatal shots."

"So?" Wire queried. "It all fits."

"Yes, but this piece might not fit." Jessa held up a photograph. "A reporter took this shot of Henry getting arrested just after the shooting. Look at his boots." She handed the picture to Lupe, seated at the next table, who in turn passed the photo to Maeve and Wire.

"What do you make of those boots?" Jessa asked.

"They look like traditional Native style to me," Mr. Chesterton offered. "High-top moccasins."

"What kind of sole do you think boots like that would have?"

"Hard to tell," Detective Kwan replied. "I'm guessing they're handmade, so could be anything."

"If I was guessing—and it would only be a guess—I'd expect rawhide leather soles," Lupe ventured.

"Think those boots really go with this print?" Jessa handed around the photo labeled "Lewis Henry shoeprint."

Wire frowned. "At first glance, I'd say no. The prints look like work boots, or hiking boots—they've got a real heavy pattern with lots of grip. Don't seem to match those fancy moccasin-boots in the picture."

"But hey, this was police work. They wouldn't goof that up," Lupe protested.

Wire scrunched up his mouth as though he were sucking a lemon. "You missed all the fun we had in LA this summer—the Neptune PD totally covered up a murder for this scum-ball politician and his hoochie girlfriend."

"That was in a big city. Folks around here wouldn't do something like that."

Wire shook his head. "These were Feds, the most powerful law enforcement in the country—dealing with a rich and powerful corporation. You know what they say about power—it corrupts."

"I get your point," Lupe conceded. "There was a lot at stake in this case."

And people can be weak. Jessa had been with Lupe and Maeve in LA when corruption had played a big role in the case they had solved.

"The evidence might have been doctored, or someone could have made a mistake." Ms. Kwan shook her head. "Remember the first OJ Simpson case? The police totally botched up the collecting and preserving of material evidence. Those sorts of things can happen, even on a big situation."

"But this Diamondback Corporation shoot-out was a long time ago," Lupe said. "If there was a mismatch, we'd never be able to prove it."

"Probably not," Ms. Kwan agreed. "But on the other hand, there *is* something we could check out. It's a slim chance, but—" She smiled at the students. "I say we give it a try."

Chapter 5
SORTING OUT THE FACTS

Whenever she felt worried, window-shopping downtown helped Jessa feel better. *I like that Rasta knit cap... wonder what they want for it?* She pressed her nose against the cold window of the outfitter's shop. Her breath made a small round cloud on the glass. Then she noticed a familiar face mirrored in the window behind her.

"Jessa Carter?"

She turned around. "Hello, Mr. Peshlaki."

His wrinkled face was brimmed by a low-crowned black hat, set-off with a turquoise-and-silver hatband. Around his neck, the Diné healer wore a huge chunk of shiny blue-green rock. His down jacket made him look stockier than his actual, spidery frame. Jessa always thought that despite his venerable years, Stanley Peshlaki—medicine man and artist—seemed youthful on the inside.

"You look different," he said. "Your hair—"

She grinned. "Yeah. White girls, you know—we change our hair color all the time."

"Diné young women do that too, now." He chuckled. "Me, I like grey. Suits me just fine."

"Mom says something about grey hair being a sign of wisdom."

"Well, I don't know about that, but it is good not to hide your age. Why should I be ashamed of something that deserves respect?" He changed the subject and said, "Funny meeting you, today. I was talking about you, just last week, with a man I visit in the big prison."

"Yeah, Lewis Henry, right?"

"You are a mind reader?"

"No, just a letter reader. Lewis and I write to each other, and he told me he had talked to you about me." She looked down at a glossy print in a frame in Mr. Peshlaki's hand. "You taking up photography?"

"Always have played with it. Not too different from painting, really—they're both all about catching Creator's work and getting it to freeze for a moment. Just the opposite from sand painting, where you create beauty and blow it all away to the Holy People. In these modern art forms, you try to preserve the loveliness."

Jessa stepped back to see the photograph better. "That's a cool effect."

"I've been playing with a laptop computer and a digital camera. Neat things you can do with computer images, nowadays."

"I think it's awesome that you're learning new ways to do art."

"I try and learn new things all the time—while keeping hold of the ancient paths, too. It can be a real balancing act."

"What do you call that picture?" she asked.

"*Electric Stallion.*"

"Cool. You going to sell it?"

He pointed at a store up the street. "Gonna put it on consignment at the Snow Owl Gallery."

"How much you asking?"

"I think a thousand dollars, for this one." He smiled. "You want to buy it?"

"Sure—I'd like to. But let's see . . . I'd have to skip lunch for the next ten years or so. Maybe I should get a job first."

He winked at her. "I've got an easier idea. Want to trade me one of your paintings?"

"You'd do that?"

"Sure. I admire your work."

"But you're a real artist. You've had shows in LA, and—"

He cut her off with a quick motion of his hand. "Just because I've had a few shows doesn't make me any better artist than you are. You capture beauty as well as I do."

"Wow." Jessa stood still, letting this unfamiliar feeling wash over her. Pride, joy, awe, humility, all swirled together in a dazzling rush of emotion. "I don't know what to say."

"Just come out to my Hogan sometime with one of your paintings and we'll swap."

She smiled, but then she thought of something. "I'm glad you're here. I've been wanting to ask you—"

"About Lewis Henry?"

She nodded. "Do you think . . . think he's innocent?"

The healer had a far-away look in his eyes. "Innocent of that shooting? Hard to say, being as how I wasn't there."

"But he says he didn't do it. Do you believe him?"

"Sometimes I can tell folks are lying, other times not. Some medicine people can tell things like that all the time—but I'm not one of them." He paused, as though he were choosing his words carefully. "All I can say is this: I tend to believe a man, unless there's a good reason not to. Lewis Henry acts like someone who's learned to walk in Hozho—in the beauty way. So I'm inclined to believe him. But then, I'm not the law. It's not for me to say—I just try and be a friend for those poor guys locked-up in the Big House."

Jessa nodded. "Thanks, Mr. Peshlaki. And I will visit you sometime soon."

"That would be great. I'd like to have one of your paintings hanging in the Hogan." The elder looked over her shoulder. "Hey, isn't that your boyfriend?"

She spun around. *Ken.* She turned back to Mr. Peshlaki. "Aah, well, he's my ex-boyfriend. As in former, in a previous life."

"Previous life wasn't so long ago. Maybe you still have some feelings?"

Jessa blushed. "Nice talking to you, Mr. Peshlaki. See you soon." She turned back toward Ken Benally. *Should I run—or face him? What's wrong with me? I'm acting like a stupid little girl.*

He was waving at her. "Hey, Jessa! I've been wanting to talk to you."

She tried not to stare into his chocolate-colored eyes. "Uh . . . what about?"

Ken pointed to the nearby entrance of the Café Paradiso coffee shop. "About the new CSC case. Got time to share a cup?"

"Aah. . ." *Why was she so tongue-tied? I just want to get away—but Ken's dad was there at the scene of the crime, and maybe he has something I need to hear.*

Ken smiled down at her. "Come on. It's wicked cold out here. Coffee'll warm you right up."

A few minutes later, Ken sat across from her in a booth, fidgeting with his cup of mocha. "You look so . . . different. I'm not sure I can get used to those red dreads."

"You don't like it?" *Why should I care? "Does it change my image?" What was it you liked about me, Ken—my body, my voice? Or the real me?*

He shook his head. "I didn't say I didn't like it. I think it's creative. Like . . . your soul."

He met her eyes, and she saw the sincerity in his gaze. She didn't want to see it, though.

"We made killer music together." He smiled, shook his head, remembering.

"Yeah. Red, White, and Blues was the best band this little town has seen. We rocked."

"And you wailed. Like Janis Joplin and Pat Benatar rolled into one."

"We coulda been something." She tried to hold back her bitterness, but it spilled out of her. "Except there was that little thing with you and Lupe after the show, and there was Veronika-with-a-K, who just happened to be all skinny and sexy so she got my place in the band."

"That's not what happened. You had quit the band—skipping all the practices."

"Because I couldn't handle being around you, after you betrayed me."

"I don't want to fight." He looked down at his coffee cup. "I still get kids asking me if we're gonna start the band again. You get those questions too?"

She shrugged. *Time to change the subject.* "So you said you wanted to talk about our new case at CSC?"

"Yeah. Sorry I've been out of things since college started—but I'm still interested."

"I hear it's a lot of work being a freshman." *He doesn't have another girl yet, does he?*

"Yeah. It's a lot of work. But I hear you're looking into the Lewis Henry case."

Does he know about his dad's role? "Yeah. Lewis says he's innocent."

Ken frowned. "Talk is cheap. Any reason to believe him?"

Why are you so interested? Is the case what's really behind this get-together? Or did you actually want to see me? Jessa nodded. "We've turned up an irregularity in the case files. This is hard to believe after all these years, but the prosecutors must have switched some forensic evidence. It's either a mistake—or they falsified things."

Ken raised an eyebrow. "Really?"

"Yeah. We went over the case files at CSC. I found a picture labeled 'Lewis Henry shoeprint,' and then a photo of the arrest. I thought the print looked unlikely to go with Henry's shoes. On a long shot, Ms. Kwan checked with the jail facility where Henry was first incarcerated. Fortunately for us, they took his boots when he was checked in, and issued prison-wear footgear in their place. Believe it or not, his high-top moccasins from a decade and a half ago have been sitting in a police custody locker all this time!"

"If they're leather, they won't be much good to him now."

"Yeah, he couldn't wear them now, even if he were released. But that's not the point." Jessa became more animated, forgetting her discomfort. "The exciting thing is—"

"The shoes and the print—"

"Don't fit. The shooter's prints have a fancy tread—and Henry was wearing old-style Navajo leather-bottom shoes when the killing happened."

"Wow." Ken stared down into his coffee mug. "Does this mean you're pursuing the case further?"

"Of course. We have a good clue that someone else stood behind Frederick Allen and pulled the trigger."

Ken took a slow sip of his coffee. "Who do you think?"

Jessa shrugged. "Maybe the company man, McClintock. Maybe someone else. We're just starting." She watched Ken's brow furrow, and she knew something was bothering him. Without thinking, she reached a hand across the table, then snatched it back. *Things are different now*, she reminded herself. *He doesn't want my comfort.*

"Why did you really want to see me?" she asked him. "You called this meeting. So what's on your mind?"

He shifted in his seat. "I told you. Just . . . ah . . . keeping up on Crime Scene Club."

"So why not meet with Maeve or Wire—or Lupe."

"Because I ran into you. And besides, you know I wouldn't just 'meet' with Lupe."

Jessa made a face. "Don't try to play me, Ken. She told me you asked her out this summer, while I was in California."

"I didn't exactly. . . she's reading into what—"

"Tell me you're not attracted to her," Jessa interrupted.

"Well, I, uh . . . she doesn't mean to me what you do . . . uh, meant to me." His face was red.

Jessa slammed her fist on the table, clattering the coffee mugs. "After all we've been through, you still can't shoot straight with me. It's a good thing I left you."

He bit his lip.

Jessa sighed. "So tell me, straight up, why did you ask to get together?"

"Mostly because . . . I miss you. I–I wish we could start over, at least a little bit."

"Come on, you're living at the university now. There's probably a dozen college girls all hot for you."

He shrugged. "They're not like you. No one is really like—"

Jessa grimaced and interrupted again. "I'll make you a little recording and title it 'sweet talk' so you can just press a button when you decide to shovel it on. You said, 'Mostly because'—so what's the other part? This isn't about romance, and it's not about a sudden renewal of interest in CSC. I don't suppose your dad has something to do with this?"

Ken looked sheepish. "I forgot what a good detective you are." He swallowed the last of his coffee. "My dad did say something the other night, about the fact that CSC had requested the files on the case. He told me he used to hang around with Act Now, back in his radical days. Guess he was near the shooting. I was curious."

"He wasn't just near—he was in the shootout, blazing away like the rest of them. Does he still own that .223 with a scope? It is a .223, isn't it? Because the prosecution seems to have had some trouble getting their facts straight."

Ken squirmed in his seat.

Jessa gave him a level look. "He told you to talk to me, didn't he?"

"Look, Jessa, I know this looks bad, but it's not like you think. I *care* about you. Laugh at me, get mad, whatever—you're still the one girl I care about, the one I wanna be with. So when Dad says, 'She doesn't know what a dangerous can of worms she's opening. Your old girlfriend could get into real trouble in this town, tampering with this case'— well, then I think, if anything happened to you and I didn't try to warn you, protect you. . . ." His voice died away.

"I *don't* need *you* to protect me!" Jessa realized she was shouting. She flashed an apologetic glance at the other patrons and lowered her voice. "You always acted like I was some cute little thing that needed your help. But I'm intelligent, I've got guts. And did more to solve crimes than you did."

"Hey, I'm not saying—"

"Just because you're a policeman's son, an athlete, and all that, don't think, don't you dare think. . . ." She broke off, too angry now to speak.

He put his hands up in a sign of surrender. "I can't win, can I?"

"Not when the facts are so obvious. Your old man gets suddenly concerned, because it wouldn't be cool for Sergeant Victor Benally, hero of the Flagstaff PD, to be all over the papers for some incident years ago when he was blasting away at an FBI agent."

"Jessa, that's not the reason—"

"What does he know that he's not telling the world? He was there, looking through a scope. What did he see? Who really killed Agent Allen?"

"You're making this way bigger than—"

"Am I?" She glared. "You tell me you love me, then you cheat on me—twice—go off to college, and then pop up in my life and act all caring, because your old man tells you to get me off this case?" She stood up. "You can pay for the coffees. I definitely think this little date should be your treat, after the way you've acted." She shouldered her purse and headed for the door.

"Jessa, please," he called after her.

She turned. "I can't believe I ever kissed you. Frankly, I'd rather lick a toilet. At least I'd know what kind of filth is inside it. With you, who can say?" She strode out the door without looking back.

Outside, she blinked away her tears. *Well, at least I'm a good actress. A few more scenes like that, I might convince even myself that I'm not in love with him anymore.*

The next day, Jessa struggled to balance her juice, tofu bar, and sprouts-and-spinach sandwich while making her way to a picnic table in the middle of campus. She spilled the food items onto the wooden surface and had just sorted them out when Maeve and her friend Sean seated themselves on the other side of the table.

"So what's happening with your Crime Scene case?" asked Sean. "You get the old dude out of jail yet?"

"His name is Lewis Henry," Jessa snapped. "And no, he's still serving his life sentence, and I'm worried because he has serious health issues."

"Jessa did some right-on detective work." Maeve bit into her double hamburger, a dab of ketchup dribbling onto her bottom lip. "She found a mistake—or a set-up—with a piece of evidence in the trial. But Ms. Kwan told us it's only a start. It'll take a lot more than that to turn his conviction around."

Jessa gave Sean a thoughtful look. "Is it weird living with an aunt who's a detective—and works part-time at the school?"

"Totally stinks," Sean admitted. "I can't get away with anything,"

"Not that he'd ever get in trouble. Sean's all goodness and light, aren't you?" Maeve smiled and pinched the boy's side.

"Hey!" He jabbed at her ribs, then they leaned against each other's forehead and giggled, their noses touching.

Do I have to watch this?

Mr. Levon, the theater teacher, walked by the table. "Maeve, Sean, why do I have to keep telling you two? Control yourselves on campus."

"Gee, Mr. L, we're just laughing," Maeve said innocently. "Since when is laughing against the rules?"

It should be, Jessa thought, if only to spare the kids who don't have someone special to flirt with. She had been trying hard to forget her conversation with Ken.

Her thoughts were interrupted when she noticed the office secretary, Ms. Garcia, headed her way. *Whoa, did I do something to get in trouble?*

"Hi, Ms. Garcia. What's up?"

The secretary looked serious. "There's a woman at the office, a Mrs. Allen, who asked if she could speak with you. I made very clear that this is school, she's not your parent, so she has no right to come here, and you can certainly choose not to speak with her, if you wish."

Maeve and Jessa glanced at one another. "The victim's widow?" Maeve muttered.

Jessa shrugged. "If this is her, she might be able to help us with some more clues. I'd better go see."

When Jessa entered the waiting room in front of the school administration office, she found a woman in her mid-forties with a pleasant face and neatly cut blond hair curling around her cheeks. Jessa caught just a hint of some pleasant perfume.

"Jessa?"

"Yes."

"I'm Ella Allen." She hesitated, as though she weren't sure how to continue.

"Mrs. Allen, I'm sorry for your loss. I can't really know how awful it is to lose a husband, but . . . I lost a good friend last year. So I can imagine a little bit how you felt."

The woman smiled. "Thank you, Jessa. Sarah Crown was your art instructor, wasn't she? I read about her murder in the papers." Ella Allen looked sad. "I have one of Sarah's paintings over my mantle."

"Really? Which one?"

"It's called *Ravens at Cathedral Rock*."

Jessa smiled, remembering. "I was in her studio when she began that one. It has the birds in kind of a figure eight, over the red rocks?"

"Yes, that's the one. I'm glad I was able to purchase it." Ella Allen seemed more at relaxed now, as though their connection through Sarah Crown had eased her discomfort. "Jessa, you're part of the Crime Scene Club at this school, right?"

"Yes."

"And I understand you correspond with—my husband's killer." The warmth in her voice faded.

"I–I exchange letters with Lewis Henry."

Ella Allen nodded. "I have friends in the federal office in Phoenix. They tell me your group has requested the documents from the trial." She took a step closer to Jessa. "Are you hoping to reopen the case?"

Jessa searched for the right words. "We're examining the case, going over the evidence. To see if there's anything that might indicate a mistake was made."

"And have you found anything like that?"

"Yes," Jessa replied. "There's something wrong with the footprint evidence used by the prosecution."

"Footprint evidence? How could something like that overturn a whole case?"

"It can't. It just . . . just means we want to keep on looking." Jessa was feeling more uncomfortable with every word.

"Do you know the pain you're causing?" It was a matter-of-fact question; Ella spoke the words without a hint of sarcasm or even bitterness.

"I'm sorry?"

"This is the third time since the trial that well-intentioned, liberal-minded folks have tried to get that murderer another hearing," Ella explained. "I'm sure you know that the Act Now organization is still around, albeit under a different name. There are even bumper stickers. Every now and then I see one—'Free Lewis Henry.'" Ella's voice trembled. "You can't know how awful it is to go through the trial, to wonder if your husband's killer is going to walk free. It's not just about justice, it's about being afraid. What if he kills again? What if he comes after me?"

Jessa put her hand on the wall to steady herself. "Mrs. Allen, I don't get the sense that Lewis Henry is a threat."

The older woman put up her hand. "I know, I've heard it all. He's very spiritual, artistic, caring." She shook her head. "Ask the head warden at the prison facility what he thinks of Lewis Henry. Or for that matter, ask the judge at the trial. They'll both tell you—Lewis Henry may not be formally educated, but he's brilliant. Smart enough to fake 'rehabilitation' in jail. Clever enough to convince the general public—not just his old pot-smokin' buddies—that he's innocent."

"Mrs. Allen, I–I didn't reopen this case to hurt you."

The other woman looked at Jessa for a moment. "Of course you didn't," she said finally. "You seem like a wonderful young lady. But—it *does* hurt me. Every time this comes back into the public spotlight, I go through the pain of it all again."

"I'm sorry. Really." She didn't know what else to say.

"Jessa, will you do me a favor?"

"I'll try."

"Will you at least think twice, before going any further? I won't insult your intelligence by telling you what to do. But I–I wanted you to understand what it's like to be a victim, and I'm asking you to keep me in mind, too. Don't just listen to Lewis Henry. Listen to the woman whose life he completely destroyed."

"I . . . I will, Mrs. Allen, I promise."

Evening of October 11

What have I got myself into? It started out simple enough, but now it's a tangled mess. The victim's widow seems like a smart, sensible woman, and she makes me wonder—how far should I trust Lewis Henry? I've been fooled by enough men before. Why should he be any different?

And what if Henry is innocent, but we can't finger the real killer? Then justice for him is justice-denied for Ella Allen. She has to live with her husband's unsolved murder.

"Truth" sounds so noble—but can we ever really know what it is? Especially a decade and a half after something happened? I was just barely born when this shootout went down. If I wasn't there, if I didn't see what happened with my own two eyes, how can I totally believe anyone's story? Maybe everyone just has their own version of the truth, but in the end nothing's completely true.

I thought I was defending innocence, like someone should have stood up for me against Randy when I was a little girl. Crazy thing is, I'm beginning to think maybe Mom wasn't so awful after all. It's hard to go against the flow. Your mind plays tricks on you when everyone has their own opinion, their own perspective. Do I really know what she was going through? Maybe she wasn't really lying so much as she was seeing the truth Randy wanted her to see, the truth she wanted to see.

But I do know my pain. That was MY truth. But it was a long time ago. And maybe a whole different thing than this case I'm on now?

I wouldn't have started this case if I knew what a mess it would be. Question is: Can I back out now? Should I?

Ms. Kwan set-up a meeting with McClintock's widow for tomorrow. Seems the company man died of a heart attack years ago, but Mrs. McClintock has agreed to talk to us. The way this case is going, I don't expect that meeting to be pretty.

Oh, well. We'll pursue this one lead—and I'll then talk to the club about giving up. My life's confusing enough without getting lost in this labyrinth.

Chapter 6
FOLLOWING THE TRUTH

"You seem awful quiet today."

Jessa turned from the squad car window toward Ms. Kwan, who was driving. She caught a scent of the policewoman's perfume, something sweet but tasteful. "Lots to think about, I guess."

"That meeting you had with Agent Allen's widow?"

"That and . . . other stuff." She didn't want to talk about Ken Benally or his father.

The police-band radio crackled; Ms. Kwan listened a moment, then turned her attention back to Jessa. "You can bow out now, if you like. I can interview Mrs. McClintock by myself."

Jessa took a deep breath. "No. I want to see it through this far. But thank you."

Ms. Kwan waved a small, neatly manicured hand. "Don't mention it."

They drove along old Route 66 in silence for a few minutes, then took a turn that led into a trailer park. Susan McClintock's home was a desert tan doublewide unit. A late-model SUV sat under a carport in front.

The door opened to Ms. Kwan's knock, and the three woman stood silently for a few seconds, sizing up each other. Mrs. McClintock was a large woman, with angular features; she appeared more curious than antagonistic. "Won't you come in?" she asked finally.

"Thank you," Detective Kwan said.

Inside, Mrs. McClintock gestured toward the sofa, a solid-looking, Southwest-fashion piece of furniture. She took a seat in an armchair facing the sofa. "What can I do for you?"

"We're reexamining the shootout at the Diamondback mine site back in 1991."

"The one my husband was in."

"That's right."

"Is the case officially reopened?"

"No, ma'am. At this point, our investigation is just a project for the Flagstaff Charter School Crime Scene Club."

"Is this another attempt to prove innocence for Lewis Henry?"

"You could say that," Detective Kwan agreed.

"Got any reason to doubt the court's findings?"

"An apparent mistake with a piece of evidence," Detective Kwan replied.

"Why do you want to talk with me?"

Jessa decided to speak up. "Mrs. McClintock, your husband was the key witness in the case."

"Heaven knows, I'm aware of that. Sat in the courtroom every day for almost two weeks. I remember every bit of it."

"We're wondering," Jessa said carefully, "if there's anything you might add to what's already in the record. Something that your husband might have told you, while he was still alive."

The large woman sighed, leaned back, and closed her eyes a moment, then sat up straighter and gazed at the two on the couch. What she said next surprised them. "I'm getting old enough that I start thinking about the end coming—and I want to leave here with a clean conscience. There's things been bothering me . . . for a long time now."

Jessa held her breath, waiting.

The widow continued, "There was nothing in the trial that didn't ring true, mind you. Everything Bob—my husband—said in court, he said the same thing to me at home.

But there were some things a bit strange, after the trial was all over." She took a breath and grasped her faded apron with her fists. "The week after the trial ended, Bob got a raise—a *big* raise. In fact, it was twice what he'd made before. He said the company was just grateful for his protection, and that sounded plausible enough. But I watch enough detective shows, and in the years since he passed away, I've gotten to wondering."

"You think the company was paying hush money?" Detective Kwan asked.

Susan McClintock shrugged. "I wouldn't think such a thing, except for something else that happened. It was about six months after the trial, and life was just settling back down. Then one evening, there was a bang on the door. Bob answered. It was a young Navajo guy, all agitated. At the time, I thought he was just a radical—the kind of people we tended to dismiss pretty easily, especially back then. But recently, I was watching the TV, and they had this police sergeant on the show—Officer Victor Benally, complete with medals on his chest. And I realized, that's him, Victor Benally is the same man as the young fellow who came to our place that night. Can you believe that former radical is an officer in our PD, now?"

"What did he say after banging on the door?" Detective Kwan asked.

"At the time, I thought he was drunk or high or something. But thinking back, and putting things together, I wonder if he wasn't just . . . angry. Outraged is the word that keeps coming to mind."

Jessa bit her lip, wishing Mrs. McClintock would get to the point.

"He was shouting," the widow continued. "I didn't hear every word. I was afraid, to be honest, so I hid in the bedroom. But I could make out most of what he said." She paused. "He was talking about 'blood money'—he said, 'How much did they pay you?' and then, 'Is that what Lewis's life is worth?'"

"How did your husband reply to all that?"

"That's the funny thing. He let the man rave for a while—a lot longer than I expected. I thought he'd threaten the man, or call the police or something. But he let Benally yell and rant. Finally Bob said, 'You done?' and the Indian went away, then."

"Did you talk to your husband about that incident, afterward?"

"I tried. But he said he was tired, and that he didn't want to say anything more. Then—just the

Schmaling Memorial
Public Library
Fulton, Illinois

week after—he had his heart attack and died." She looked at the floor, and her face seemed to sag with the weight of all the years she had lived without her husband.

"Mrs. McClintock, I know this is hard, but I have to ask," Dorothy Kwan probed carefully, "was Bob the kind of man who . . . might falsify his story in court?"

Jessa's breath caught in her throat.

"I surely don't want to disrespect my departed husband." Mrs. McClintock's voice wobbled. "He was a good man—faithful—for almost thirty years." She looked down at her large, knob-knuckled hands as they twisted her apron. "But there was a part of him he kept guarded. I guess he was the strong, silent type, you know? I always felt like there was a big distance between us. He had his demons, I think . . . but he never discussed them. Not with me."

She drew in a breath and squared her broad shoulders. "If Bob lied in that courtroom, he did it because of something he believed in. Maybe it was the company—he was very loyal to Diamondback, his whole life. Maybe it was his concern for me, his need to be a good provider. You can't imagine how we struggled. He was in the war, and he got a little money from the government. But he never finished high school, and that made things hard. So he never earned enough. We always lived in dumpy old shacks and drafty mobile homes. Diamondback didn't pay security guards much. Fact is, we never made ends meet, until after that trial, and then the big checks started coming."

"Do they still come?" Jessa asked.

Susan McClintock nodded. "Got one day before last."

"Aren't you afraid that, talking to us. . . ?"

Mrs. McClintock shook her head. "Doesn't matter now. Comes a time when a clean conscience means more than money."

"Would you be willing to tell a judge everything you just told us?" Detective Kwan asked.

"I would. Mind you, I don't *know* that Bob wasn't telling the truth. The company could just appreciate his bravery, like he said. That Indian could have been tanked up that night and talking nonsense. There's no way to prove anything now, after all these years."

Jessa sat up straighter. "Mrs. McClintock, by any chance—I know this sounds crazy, but—would you happen to still have the boots that your husband wore on the day of the incident?"

The older woman thought for a moment. "Why, yes. I left a pile of his things in that shed just out back. His rain slicker, his Stetson, and his work boots. I suspect they're pretty moldy."

"Could we borrow them?"

"Don't know why not." She pushed herself to her feet.

Jessa sensed that Ms. Kwan was struggling to restrain her excitement. "Speaking of things you didn't want to get rid of," the detective said, "do you by chance have the gun he used for his security work?"

Mrs. McClintock gave a quick nod. "Just a moment." She went into an adjoining room and returned a moment later with a fancy-looking rifle. "If this and the boots will help you get to the bottom of what happened, you're free to keep them long as you like."

"Thank you," the detective replied. "I'll write out a receipt for the loan of these items." Detective Kwan hesitated, looking thoughtful. "Mrs. McClintock, I want you to know—you don't have to do this. It's possible—I can't say how likely, but there is a chance—that these items could be evidence implicating your departed husband in . . . some dishonesty."

"Bob's met his Maker already. We were both baptized in the Temple, but it takes more than ceremonies. It takes a good heart to be raised with the righteous on that final day. So it's like I told you, I want to see that whatever scores there may be are settled, while there's still time on this earth for me to do that."

"I wish there were more people like you, Mrs. McClintock." Detective Kwan smiled. "It takes real courage to face the truth, no matter what it is."

Mrs. McClintock waved a large hand, as though the detective's compliment was a pesky fly she was shooing. "But there's one more thing I need to say before you go."

Jessa and Ms. Kwan waited while she gathered her thoughts.

"Detective, I can see you're capable of handling whatever comes your way," she said finally, glancing at the .38 holstered on Ms. Kwan's waist. "But young lady, I'm a bit concerned on your account." She looked into Jessa's face. "The men that run Diamondback, I wouldn't call them evil, exactly. I'm grateful for how they've provided for me all these years. But I sure wouldn't want to get on their bad side. That company is named right, seems to me. They're dangerous, like a diamondback rattler. Anyone gets in their way, they somehow manage to eat 'em right up. I'd hate to be a teenager and have the company boys against me."

Jessa couldn't find any words to answer the older woman. She couldn't say she wasn't scared—because she was.

Ms. Kwan put a hand on Jessa's shoulder. "Jessa and I will talk about that, Mrs. McClintock. We greatly appreciate your candor, about everything."

As they drove away from the trailer, Jessa glanced over her shoulder at the boots and rifle in the back seat. "Think those will tell us something?"

"They're prime forensic evidence. Even after all these years—they could tell us a great deal."

"Mrs. McClintock, she's a cool lady, isn't she?"

"She's special, all right," the detective agreed. "Jessa, what she said about Diamondback. How do you feel about that?"

Jessa hesitated. "It doesn't make things any easier," she said finally.

Detective Kwan sighed. "No, it doesn't. I keep trying to keep you CSC members safe, but somehow—"

"We just find trouble."

Ms. Kwan nodded. "Jessa, you will be careful?"

"Of course."

But after what I just heard, I'm not ready to quit the case. Sometimes you just have to follow the truth—even when it scares you.

Chapter 7
THE SHOE FITS

"Now *this* is what Crime Scene Club is all about."

Jessa couldn't help but smile at Wire's enthusiasm. He usually seemed so disinterested in the world outside his own extraordinary mind. Now, absorbed with technical gadgets, he was transformed.

Wire had taken digital photographs of the bottom of McClintock's boots and loaded the images onto his laptop. Now, he was toggling two windows: one showed a close-up of the crime scene photo labeled "Lewis Henry shoeprint," the other was the image he had just taken.

"You're creepy, Wire." Maeve was leaning on a counter with a bored expression. "Don't you get turned on by anything normal?"

"*I'm* creepy?'" Wire chuckled, his gaze still glued to the computer monitor. "You should talk, Maeve. I heard about when you and Sean got caught in the parking lot, with those fake fangs."

"Shut up, Dork."

Wire grinned.

"Hey, everyone gets their kicks in their own way." Jessa tried to smooth things over.

"Enough." Mr. Chesterton sighed. "We're probing a case here, remember? Got a match on those shoe prints yet, Wire?"

"Hold on. Almost done." He punched keys, and the two windows on the screen slid over, one on top of the other; the two images rotated slightly, one of the shoe print photos expanded to match the other's size, and then— "They're identical," Wire pronounced. "The shoe fits."

Mr. Chesterton whistled. "What the prosecutor labeled as 'Lewis Henry shoeprint'—"

"Was, in fact, Robert McClintock's boot," Jessa concluded. "They mixed up the evidence." She pulled a paper out of a file folder. "And this little diagram, which was drawn by the prosecutor, shows a definite pattern with the boot prints, the victim's body, and the trajectory of the bullet."

"Judging from these items of evidence," Wire concluded, "it was McClintock, not Henry, who shot that FBI agent."

"Why?" Maeve asked. "The FBI was on Diamondback's side."

"Maybe we've been looking too narrowly," Mr. Chesterton suggested. "What happened *after* the trial ended?"

"Public opinion turned against the Act Now group," Maeve answered. "People saw them as murderers. So Diamondback opened their mine with no trouble."

"The whole thing makes sense," Wire agreed. "Diamondback hired their security guy to murder the FBI agent and pin it on the radicals. It was a gutsy move—downright Machiavellian—but it paid off for them; swayed public support in their direction."

"Macchia-a-what?" Maeve asked.

Hey, I know this! "Machiavelli was a prince that lived . . . uh, a long time ago. He believed that politicians should hold power by lying to their subjects all the time," Jessa explained.

"Well, duh." Maeve rolled her eyes. "What else would you expect from politicians? Why did someone have to make up a big word to explain that leaders lie?"

The door opened, and Lupe came in with Detective Kwan. "You won't believe what we found," Lupe blurted.

"We've got pretty exciting news here, too." Jessa quickly told them about the shoe prints.

"In that case," Detective Kwan said, "the deceased Mr. McClintock is declared guilty—by two pieces of hard evidence."

"*Two* pieces?"

"The stuff that the FBI sent us included the two bullets that killed Agent Allen," Lupe explained. "It was kind of frightening, touching them."

"I think it would be cool," Maeve said.

Lupe ignored her. "Back in 1991, the FBI's ballistic expert declared that 'the slug is badly damaged . . . the rifling too corrupted for a positive match.' But that's not what our local ballistics guy told Ms. Kwan and me, just half-an-hour ago."

The detective explained. "We shot a few rounds from McClintock's old rifle into the water tank, and then compared those with the slugs from the murder weapon. Despite what someone said at the trial—"

"They match," Lupe concluded, so excited that her voice squeaked.

"We've got the murderer." Maeve shot her fist into the air. "It was Diamondback's guy. The shoe fits, and so does the bullet."

"The 'smoking gun' was a lie," Mr. C added.

"Lewis Henry is innocent. Now he can go free." Jessa's eyes filled with tears.

"Club, I hate to rain on your parade," Ms. Kwan said crisply, "but this case is a long way from overturned." The others stared at her. "Five people, all in this room, know what really happened. If it were up to us, Lewis Henry would be released tomorrow. But it's not up to us. There needs to a complete retrial of the case. It's not easy to get a judge to agree to that. Running a government murder case takes a great amount of money and time. We're going to need a lawyer—or more likely, a team of lawyers— good ones. And that kind of legal expertise costs a small fortune."

"There are a couple of law professors at the university who've taken on innocence cases," Mr. Chesterton said. "I could try and meet with them."

"Excellent idea," Ms. Kwan agreed. "Though I wouldn't hold my breath."

"We need publicity," Lupe declared.

"Huh?" Jessa asked.

"She's right." Wire spoke in his customary monotone. "Innocence cases are all about public perception."

"But we have *evidence* . . . and the facts don't lie. We have the *truth*."

"Doesn't matter—people do lie," said Maeve. "Lupe's right. It may be the twenty-first century, but a lot of people still get freed or get fried based on public perception. We need some kind of campaign to let the public know what we've learned about this case."

"Art!" Jessa practically shouted.

"What?" Maeve looked at her as though she'd lost her mind.

"We can do an art exhibition, right here on campus," Jessa explained. "We'll get paintings. I'll do a few original pieces, portraying the crime—in a symbolic style. Wire can do computer images, and we can combine those with huge blow-up pictures of the crime evidence. This is an artist's town, so we open an exhibition. We'll arrange the whole display so it's crystal clear what happened—and that Lewis Henry is innocent."

"We'll have a petition there, for people to sign." Lupe was catching Jessa's enthusiasm. "And we can give away bumper stickers."

"Whoa, slow down," Mr. Chesterton cautioned. "This is pretty radical."

Ms. Kwan's brow was furrowed in thought. "Lupe's right about the need for publicity. I've committed my life to forensic science because it's objective—but I've seen cases lost because of the tide of popular opinion. Yes, we need to do something to get the facts to the public. But . . . an art exhibition? That could be really controversial."

"It's edgy. Let's do it," Maeve pleaded.

"I can talk to my art teacher—I know he'll go for it," Jessa added.

"Count me in for computer graphics," Wire added.

"I don't know." Detective Kwan shook her head. "Diamondback will be all over us. They'll complain to the school board and the police department, probably try and get our club shut down."

"So? There's been authorities trying to kill CSC since we started," Lupe pointed out. "They haven't succeeded yet."

"What about Mrs. McClintock?" Detective Kwan asked. "Acquittal for Lewis Henry will only come at the cost of a conviction—for her deceased husband. He may be gone, but that's an awful heavy burden she will have to carry the rest of her life."

Jessa thought a moment. "She strikes me as a really strong woman," she said slowly, "and totally straightforward. I think she wants the truth to come out—whatever it is. She wouldn't have given us those pieces of evidence if she didn't mean for us to follow this case all the way to its conclusion."

"Agreed," the detective replied. "But let me talk to her—privately—before you get this art thing going."

Mr. Chesterton was shaking his head. "It's an awfully big risk. How do you think the media will respond?"

"They'll love it," Maeve replied. "The television and newspaper folks are totally Macchi-a-belgian."

"Machiavellian," Wire corrected.

"Whatever. Give 'em a story with murder and conspiracy, they'll be all over it like bats on blood."

"Interesting phrase." Detective Kwan grimaced, then turned to Jessa. "You opened this can of worms, and it looks like you're leading the charge for publicity. That may mean opposition will focus on you. You've had a traumatic year already. Are you ready to battle for this cause?"

Jessa grinned. "Bring it on."

I think.

Letter to Miss Jessa Carter, from State Penitentiary Prisoner #37928

October 20

Yaateh, Jessa.

Your letter floored me. I hardly know what to say.

The first time I heard about someone trying to free me, I got excited. I even dared to think that something would happen and my conviction would be overturned. That was twelve years ago.

Then there was a celebrity lawyer in California, said he'd take up my case. They were making a documentary movie with some big actors, about cases of injustice against Native people. I think the lawyer wanted to look good and seem all involved in my case so he could be in the documentary. The movie sold pretty good. Boy, was that exciting. "Somebody's going to work to get me free," I said.

Never heard from the lawyer after that. The movie came and went, and I guess he had other things to do besides work for an old Indian that can't pay him a thing.

Then, years later, your letter came. I'm amazed. You and your friends in the crime club have come up with the hard evidence that's been hidden all these years. Evidence that could free me. My hand is shaking, makes it hard to write these words.

Free. Honestly, I'm scared to think about it. I'm not sure if I should dare to hope.

Last week, I went into diabetic shock. Fell down in my cell, passed right out. I hear that Carlos screamed and screamed and banged on the steel wall with the holes in it. Guards told him "shut up." He kept yelling and banging till they finally looked in and saw me on the floor. Then they had to get a whole squad in riot gear because they always assume that a prisoner passed out on the floor is a fake, an attempt to escape.

Well, the guards came in with their shields and helmets, and by golly it's real.

So they rush me to the infirmary. When I finally come to, the doctor here says I almost bought it. In another couple of minutes I would have been dead.

And then, next day, your letter came, telling about how you're doing this exhibit and showing the evidence to try and get me pardoned. And I think, maybe that's why Grandfather didn't let me die. Maybe I will get free of this place, see the storm clouds over the mesas, and smell sage again.

I'm a jumble of emotions. I need to restore inner harmony. Will I truly be free of this cell? Thanks to you, I dare to dream of freedom again.

But all shall happen as Creator wills.

Your friend,
Lewis Henry

Chapter 8
THE EXHIBITION

Jessa hovered nervously at the outskirts of the art exhibit, watching the guests. She glanced at the displays covering the walls of the Flagstaff Charter School art room. With only two weeks to work on them, Jessa had managed to produce three enormous canvases: two pastels and a watercolor. One showed an enormous face of Lady Justice—blindfolded, but peeking through one eye—and the other pastel was a large picture of Mr. Henry's face, staring directly at the viewer. The watercolor was a smaller portrait of a young Lewis Henry, covered with red spatters like blood, over enormous black letters that formed the words "Prisoner #37928."

Jessa was proud of her paintings, but she was even more excited about a small artwork that hung in the middle of the opposite wall, a bright light shining on it: Lewis Henry's painting, titled *Smoky Mesa*. This piece was very important, apart from its artistic merit. After this night, no one would be able to think of Lewis Henry as a murderer; they would know he was an artist, with a soul.

In the middle of the room, mounted on large kiosks, were Wire's large-scale renderings of the crime scene: big, computer-graphic pictures, with life-size photographs of the footprints and blown-up images of the bullets superimposed on them.

It's a nice combination, Jessa thought. *My art speaks to the heart, Wire's computer graphics go for the head. Between us, the public should be convinced.*

She could overhear snatches of conversation: "Can you believe this? The shoeprints were switched. . . ." "This looks like real proof. . . ." "I thought it was just the left-wing crazies that wanted Henry freed, but after this. . . ."

Jessa smiled.

Lupe came up beside her. "Hey. What do you think of our show?"

"I think we're getting support for the cause."

"You bet." Lupe grinned. "Maeve's got at least twenty signatures at the table."

"Awesome."

As Lupe went to check on the punch, Jessa noticed a Native woman, heavyset, perhaps a few years older than herself. *She has a kind face,* Jessa thought. The woman was staring at two enlarged photos that showed how the bullet from McClintock's gun matched the slugs that killed Agent Allen.

Jessa walked over to the young woman. "What do you think of the display?"

The woman looked up from the display. "You're Jessa Carter, the student who started all this, am I right?"

"Yes. I don't believe we've met."

"I–I . . . some other time." The young woman spun on her heels and hurried toward the door.

What was that all about it?

Jessa didn't have long to think about it, because she spied another familiar face: Ella Allen. Jessa was about to retreat when the woman caught her eye.

"Jessa!"

Darn. "Uh, hello, Mrs. Allen." As she drew closer, she noticed the older woman was trembling. "Are you all right?"

Ella Allen gave her a wobbly smile. "Just emotional, that's all."

Jessa tried to think of the right thing to say. "I'm sorry, I tried to put down this case, but—"

"But you found all this evidence." Ella made a sweeping gesture toward the displays.

Jessa nodded.

"It looks pretty conclusive."

"Yes. I had suspicions before, but now we have proof." She lifted her head. "I think we finally know the truth."

"Jessa, I want to say—"

"I'm sorry, Mrs. Allen. I didn't want to hurt you, but I believe the truth needed to be revealed and—"

"Please," Ella Allen interrupted. "Let me finish. I want to say how thankful I am for what you've done."

"Really?"

"Absolutely. My husband was a good man, and the last thing he would ever want is an innocent soul suffering for his murder."

Jessa let out the breath she'd been holding.

"You've begun a good work here," Ella Allen continued. "I've signed the petition to get a pardon for Lewis Henry, and I also signed up to help work for his freedom until that's accomplished."

Jessa smiled. "Thank you."

"No, Jessa—thank *you*. I believe my husband is resting more peacefully now, because of what you've done."

Sarah Crown's face flashed in front of Jessa's mind's eye. "I seem to have a talent of setting things straight for . . . the dead," she said softly.

"Well, bless you. Keep it up. It's never too late to speak the truth."

Jessa slept late the next morning, and had to pedal furiously to reach school in time. As she drew closer, she could hear the faint sound of sirens ahead. By the time she reached the school, panting, a pair of gleaming red fire trucks were pulling up next to the art building.

"Oh, no." Bypassing the parking lot, she pedaled faster and leaped off her bike just outside the building.

"You can't go in there," a fire woman yelled at her. "Too dangerous!"

"But my display—"

"Sorry, girl, it's all gone up in flames."

Jessa collapsed on her knees, staring through the door at smoldering piles of ash. She felt a hand on her shoulder. "I'm sorry," Maeve said in her ear.

"All that work—" Jessa whispered.

"Was worth it," Wire's voice concluded.

"He's right," Maeve said. "We got the word out. You started another kind of fire with this exhibit, one that won't be so easily extinguished. I've got half a hundred signatures, and that's just the start of our petition."

"Jessa, you all right?" Mr. Chesterton joined the group.

"No. But . . . I'll bounce back."

Mr. C's normally cheerful face was grim. "We've got someone's attention, all right."

"They're sending us a message," Maeve agreed.

Mr. Chesterton frowned. "I just hope this is the worst of it."

"What are you going to be for Halloween tomorrow?" Jessa asked Maeve a few days later during lunch.

"Myself."

The three girls laughed. "Lupe, what about you?"

"Wonder Woman."

Maeve looked her up and down. "Aren't you a bit scrawny?"

Lupe stuck her tongue out, then looked up as Wire joined their table. "Wire, what about you? What are you going to be for Halloween?"

"No time to dress up. There's a big RPG tournament, five thousand dollar stakes."

"Wow." Jessa was impressed. "What will you do if you win that?"

"Buy more gear."

"As if you don't already own the best computer system in the county." Lupe laughed. "So Jessa, how about you? What are you going to be for Halloween?"

"I'll be Joan of Arc, if I can finish the outfit in time."

"She didn't have dreadlocks," Maeve shot back.

"How do you know?"

Maeve gave an evil smile. "She would of burned quicker."

Before Jessa could respond, she noticed that Mrs. Garcia was once more coming her way. "Which one of us is in trouble this time?" she muttered.

"Jessa," the office assistant called, "Detective Kwan is here to see you."

The group exchanged glances. Jessa shrugged, and headed for the office. She found Ms. Kwan seated at the desk in front of the office, an inscrutable look on her face.

"What's happening, Ms. K?"

"I just got word this morning, and I drove over to tell you personally."

"What?"

"The DA's office called. They've granted Lewis Henry a retrial."

"Yes!" Jessa jumped up and down. "He's going to be free!"

"We don't know that yet," the detective cautioned. "After all there's got to be a whole new case."

"But with the evidence we've found, don't you think...?"

"Honestly?"

"Yes." Jessa braced herself for whatever Ms. Kwan said.

The detective smiled. "I don't think we can lose."

"Wow." Jessa sat down, suddenly overwhelmed. *I did it. I gave a voice to the voiceless—and people listened!* "Can I tell the other CSC kids?"

"Of course!"

Hours later, when Jessa turned her bicycle's handlebars toward her driveway, she saw a familiar woman walking toward her door, the Native girl she had seen at the art show. "Hey!" Jessa called. "You were at the exhibition. But you left so fast."

The young woman looked down at her feet. "I'm sorry. I have trouble talking to strangers. But I was hoping to find you here, today."

"Why?"

She answered in a voice so quiet that Jessa had to strain to hear her. "I'm Alison Henry. Lewis Henry is . . ." Her round face was pink, as though she were overcome with emotion, and she seemed unable to continue. But Jessa suddenly knew what she was trying to say.

"He never told me he had a daughter! You heard the news?"

The young woman nodded. "My mother told me." She bit her lip and looked back at her feet.

"Well, hey—aren't you happy?" Jessa was confused. *She doesn't look very excited about getting her father back.*

"Actually, I've decided to leave the house. I'm moving to Phoenix, where I'll feel safe. But I wanted to talk to you before I go."

"You're leaving your home, when your dad will be coming back?" Jessa didn't understand.

"I was only eight when he went to prison. I was glad when they locked him up."

Jessa struggled to absorb that last sentence. "You . . . were *glad*?"

Alison's eyes drifted from her feet to the sidewalk. "He always used to beat me."

"Lewis—your father . . . he did *that*?" Jessa almost fell over on her bicycle. She stepped off the seat and steadied herself on the frame.

"Yeah. He would get drunk and . . . be awful." She glanced up quickly at Jessa, then darted her eyes away. "My mom was too afraid of him to do anything, so she just let him. . . . I guess it's hard to believe if . . . you didn't have that kind of problems growing up."

Jessa took a breath, trying to gather her thoughts. "I'm sorry Alison. I–I did . . . have problems like that."

"Oh." The other woman looked into Jessa's face and frowned. "You must be surprised, knowing that you've defended a child-abuser."

Jessa let the bicycle fall over onto the grass. She felt like her head was exploding.

"I'm sorry," she heard Alison say. "You're upset. This isn't why I wanted to speak to you."

Jessa forced herself to meet the other woman's eyes.

"All my life," Alison Henry continued, "I've been afraid to tell people who my father is. I would tell them, 'He died in an accident.' I don't like to tell untruths—it isn't the harmony way—but it was better than the awful facts."

"I don't blame you. I'd do the same," Jessa told her.

"So the other night, when I saw your exhibit at the school—saw the evidence, the footprints and the bullet markings—it changed my whole world, all at once. My father is an awful man, a drunk and an abuser. I don't ever want to see him again. But thanks to you, Jessa, I know the truth. I know he isn't a murderer."

Alison Henry walked away, and Jessa stared after her. Then, slowly, she pulled her bicycle up from the lawn, put it in the garage, and went into the house. She collapsed on her bed and buried her face in the pillow. *So much for the truth. . .*

Hours later, Jessa awoke when her mother came home.

"Jessa, honey, are you sick?"

"Yeah, kinda."

"I have all sorts of herbs. What are your symptoms?"

"Not that sort of sick, Mom. Just upset. I don't really want to talk about it."

Her mother hesitated in the doorway of Jessa's room. "Okay," she said finally. "I understand. I didn't want to talk to my mom when I was your age, either. But if you ever need to, Jessa—"

"Mom?" *It's an unbelievably awful day already—so why not go for broke?*

"Yes?"

"There is something else I'd like to talk about. Something I've wanted to talk about for years."

Her mother sat down on the end of Jessa's bed. "Uh-oh." She squared her shoulders. "What is it, Jessa?"

"When I was like seven or eight, and Randy lived with us—" In her mind, Jessa again saw that stinky checkered shirt, heard the gruff voice, saw that monster of a man with his gigantic hands. She took a quick, deep breath, then rushed her words, making sure she got out the terrible thoughts before she could change her mind. "You knew how he treated me. Why did you let him?"

Her mother's lip trembled.

"Why, Mom? Why?"

Her mother still said nothing.

"Answer me!" Jessa screamed.

Finally, her mother said softly, her voice broken, "Jessa, baby, I . . ." She made a choked noise and fell silent.

The silence in the room felt as though it were charged with electricity, as though lightning might suddenly flash and kill them both. Then Jessa's mother began to cry. Jessa listened to her. Slowly, the tension inside her eased. After a moment, she put a hesitant hand on her mother's shoulder.

Her mother raised a tear-stained face. "I'm not fit to be your mother. I'm a disgrace. I was weak, so weak . . . and selfish. Ever since, I've thought about it. What he did to you, what I . . . let . . . him do. I don't blame you if you hate me. I hate myself, most of the time. It's just when I'm stoned that I can look myself in the mirror, get dressed, go out. . . ."

"Mom." Jessa put her arms around her mother's shoulders and buried her face in the sweet patchouli-and-pot scent. She found herself seeing other images from that time of abuse: the look on her mother's face, desperate, frightened. *She was afraid of him, too—just like I was.* "Mom, you're being too hard on yourself."

"No. I'm not." She sobbed again. "I let him hurt you . . . the most precious thing in my life. What kind of mother would do that?"

Jessa thought about it for a moment. "An imperfect mother," she said at last. "A young woman who was broke and scared. But Mom—we're all messed up one way or another. We all let each other down. That doesn't mean we don't love each other. Or that we don't keep trying. We just have to . . . we just have to face the truth about ourselves."

"Oh, Jessa. I've made so many awful mistakes. That's the truth I haven't wanted to face."

She hugged her mother closer. "Mom," she whispered in her ear, "here's another truth: I forgive you."

Mother and daughter held each other tight, sobbing tears of both pain and relief.

Evening of October 30

I keep hearing that old Dylan tune, "A Simple Twist of Fate." And I keep thinking about the twists in this case of Lewis Henry. What if I had never written to prisoner # 37928?

Ella Allen would have gone on, secure in the mistaken belief that her husband's killer was in jail.

Susan McClintock would have gone on receiving fat checks from Diamondback, compensation for a guilty conscience that could follow her to the grave.

And Alison Henry would think that her father was in jail, getting what he deserved for what he did to her. But she'd also believe she was the daughter of a murderer. And that would haunt her.

Would justice be better served if Lewis Henry stays in jail, even though he's not a murderer? After all, I want Randy in jail. What's the difference?

No wonder Mom does so much pot. If you really get to thinking, it's enough to make you crazy. But there's one thing I know: Someone did stand up for little Jessa, so awfully mistreated in her childhood.

I stood up for her tonight.

After talking to Mom, something that's been hurting inside for a long time feels like it's mending. But I can't go to school tomorrow. There's too much confusion inside my head. How on earth can I ever tell Crime Scene Club, "We've cleared a man of murder—but I still want him punished for his other crimes"? I think I'll hop a bus to Sedona and hang out, somewhere I can chill, focus, heal.

Chapter 9
HALLOWEEN

Jessa didn't have time to finish the Joan of Arc costume. It didn't matter because she didn't feel like going to the school dance anyway. She could imagine Maeve and Lupe and Sean having a good time. Good for them. There would be plenty of other occasions to hang out with them another time.

The bus back from Sedona dropped her off just below the railroad tracks, and she walked past clusters of children dressed as ghosts and witches and hobos, on her way through downtown toward her home. Passing Café Paradiso, she was surprised to see Stanley Peshlaki, seated at a small round table with Ken Benally. The older man saw her and motioned for her to come in.

Oh, all right. Some warm coffee would feel good.

"Hello, Jessa," the medicine man greeted her.

"Hello, Mr. Peshlaki."

"You heard about Lewis Henry?"

"Yes."

"You don't look so thrilled."

"I . . . I learned some more about him. His daughter came to see me."

"Oh." Mr. Peshlaki nodded. "She has reasons to be angry at her father."

"You knew about that? And you let us go ahead with reopening his case?"

"He hasn't always been a good man. But after the evidence the Crime Scene Club found, it's obvious he is not a murderer. You kids did the right thing."

"But—people who abuse their children, they deserve to be locked up."

"Do you know what it's been like for him, in prison for all these years? Can you say for sure he hasn't suffered enough for the wrong he has done?"

Jessa frowned, trying to understand what Mr. Peshlaki was telling her.

"I don't know the answer to that question," he continued. "I'm just asking it. But Jessa, if it makes a difference, I can tell you: people can change—and Lewis Henry *has* changed. Alcohol can make a monster of any man, but he's been a long time sober now. His past torments him, but I believe he will leave prison a better man."

Jessa stared down at her hands. She was aware of Ken sitting across from her, sipping his coffee, but she could not bring herself to look at him. "I wish I could believe you."

"Life is full of mysteries, so you're bound to be confused. The truth is very hard to see sometimes. But I am proud of you, Jessa Carter, and I hope you can feel proud of yourself." He set down his coffee mug and stood. "I have to get to the train station. I'm visiting my daughter and granddaughter in Los Angeles."

Ken jumped to his feet. "I'll take you."

"Oh, no. It's just a few blocks from here. Don't tell me you don't think I'm fit enough for a short hike?"

Ken shrugged and looked uncomfortable. The medicine man laughed. "I walk twelve miles every day, from Devil's Canyon to White Bird Mesa and back. I'm as healthy as you are."

Ken grinned. "I don't doubt it."

"Have a good trip, Mr. Peshlaki," Jessa called as he strode out the door.

Jessa and Ken stared at one another. The silence between them felt suddenly heavy, as though it were weighted with unspoken words.

"Can I get you a coffee?" he asked, and she nodded.

A few minutes later, he returned with a steaming cup. "I've been wanting to talk to you," he said as handed her the mug.

"You sure? You might not like what I have to say."

"Well, I know it must be hard sitting with a guy who's more disgusting than a toilet bowl."

Her face reddened, but Ken smiled. "My dad and I talked earlier this evening. He checked in with some of his old Act Up friends and—"

"This doesn't sound so good."

"Wait. Let me finish. One of them actually works for Diamondback now."

"No way!"

"For real. After a couple of decades being ticked off, this guy decided the big energy company wasn't so bad for the Rez. Dad and him talked about the Lewis Henry retrial. This guy has friends on the board of the company. He says there were some hot-head employees that torched the school, but they weren't acting for the company. In fact, they've been fired."

"Really?"

"I kid you not. As for the big bosses at Diamond-back, they don't think there'll be any serious repercussions to reopening the case. Stuff that happened that long ago is water under the bridge. You won't believe this, but they're even thinking about paying for Henry's attorneys."

"You're right, I don't believe it."

"It's true. They think that backing a Native activist will help their reputation on the Navajo Nation."

"So they're gonna do the right things—stop harassing us and help Lewis Henry—for their own selfish reasons."

"I guess that's how the world works."

"Guess so."

Ken looked thoughtful. "I don't blame you for being sore at me. In fact, I want to offer an apology . . . and a—uh—suggestion."

"Start with the apology. I'll decide if I'm ready for the other."

"All right." He swallowed. "I was wrong—totally wrong—to let my father influence me to talk to you about that case."

"That is only the tip of the iceberg when it comes to what you have to apologize for."

"I know." He looked suitably chagrined. "I've been dishonest, unfaithful—a real loser in every way."

"True."

"I can be smart when it comes to crime work, or sports, but . . . my emotions are a mess. I don't understand myself."

Jessa smiled. "Now you're being honest." She took a sip of the hot drink. "So—you had a suggestion?"

"Yeah. I've been thinking about the band."

"Thinking?"

"The band should get together, just for a trial period. Say we rehearse for a month, and do performances for the two weeks after. Then we can decide if we want to continue."

"I don't know, the way things went down—"

"And you be the leader," Ken added.

Her eyes widened. "But that's your band. You're the leader."

"Some leader I've been. The band broke up—uh, we broke up—all because of me. Besides, you know more about music than I do."

"Wow. First time you've admitted that."

He shrugged. "Honesty might become habit forming." He reached inside his jacket pocket, pulled out something, and handed it to her.

She recoiled from the object. "Ken, I'm *not* putting your ring back on. Not after—"

"Please?" he interrupted.

She picked up the ring and cradled it in her palm. "I'm sorry. Maybe some day, but—I can only forgive so much, so fast. And I'm dealing with a lot right now."

He took the ring back, put it in his pocket. "I'll just keep hold of it—until you're ready."

"Ken, I can't promise you that I'll ever be ready."

"I know. It's okay." Ken sighed, then raised his coffee mug and said, "Let's toast."

"With coffee?"

"Why not?"

"All right." Jessa grinned. "What are we toasting?"

"Here's to the best band in Flagstaff—in the past and in the future."

They tapped their cups together.

"And another toast," Ken said. "To the best singer—and the best detective—I've ever met."

"No." She set her cup on the table. "That doesn't seem right."

"Okay, Jessa, you make a toast."

She raised her mug. "Here's to broken people—us and all the others. May they find peace, and healing, and . . . forgiveness."

The cups clinked.

As Jessa looked up, she caught her reflection in the window. *Red isn't the real me. I guess I'll let my natural color grow back. From now on, I'm gonna be true to myself.*

FORENSIC NOTES

CRIME SCENE CLUB, CASE #8

CHAPTER 1

Evidence List

Vocab Words

peers	practical
karmic	classic
perps	sleuths
legendary	stereotyping
prosperity	monotone
authentic	distinct
sacred	hypothetical
shrines	heinous

Deciphering the Evidence

When Jessa thinks about her *peers* she's thinking about the people her age, who are equal to her in some way.

In Jessa's mind, Detective Kwan offers her life *karmic* balance; in other words, Ms. Kwan brings good qualities to Jessa's life that offset some of the bad ones.

When Maeve speaks of "*perps*," she's referring to perpetrators, the people responsible for a crime.

Detective Kwan's comment that *legendary* figures have left their footprints for *posterity* means that people who are so famous that their lives have become the stuff of legend have left their footprints for future generations to appreciate.

Not everyone believes that the footprints attributed to Buddha, Mohammed, and Jesus are *authentic*; in other words, they may not be genuine or actual.

Footprints of religious leaders are displayed in *sacred shrines*, special places set aside where people can connect with the spiritual world.

Crime-solving is a more *practical* application for footprints; in other words, it is more useful than revering celebrity footprints.

Footprint analysis is a *classic* technique used by many *sleuths*. It is a traditional, well-known method used by people who solve mysteries.

Lupe wonders if footprints offer clues that are all that *credible* or believable.

When Maeve protests that Lupe is *stereotyping* her, she means that Lupe is making assumptions based on her appearance, sex, or race.

Wire speaks in a *monotone*, a low, even tone with little emotion.

After months of walking in identical pairs of shoes, Wire points out, two people will create footprints that are *distinct*—unique, separated in some way from all others.

Wire argues about the boot print taken from Maeve's *hypothetical* crime, because if it were from a real case and not a made-up, "just-suppose" scenario, he thinks she would be more careful than to walk in mud.

Detective Kwan shows the Crime Scene Club that even a careful criminal can't get away with a *heinous* crime; the right forensic techniques reveal hidden marks of the terrible activity.

Who Was Sherlock Holmes?

Sherlock Holmes is the famous fictional detective created by Sir Arthur Conan Doyle (1859-1930). Holmes first appeared in 1887 in *A Study in Scarlet*, but did not become popular until 1890 with the publication of a series of short stories called *The Adventures of Sherlock Holmes*. In the stories, Sherlock Holmes lived in London at 221B Baker Street. Holmes was a private detective, and was usually accompanied on his cases by his friend and assistant Dr. John H. Watson. Holmes is famous for his pipe, his magnifying glass, and his hat, as well as his scientific observations and deductive reasoning.

When Was the Victorian Age?

The Victorian Age was the period of time during which Queen Victoria ruled the United Kingdom. Queen Victoria reigned from 1837 to 1901, the longest reign in British history. The Victorian Age was also a time marked by many dramatic social, political, cultural, scientific, economic, and industrial changes.

The World of Forensics

Our English word "forensic" comes from the Latin word *forensis*, which means "forum"—the public area where in the days of ancient Rome a person charged with a crime presented his case. Both the person accused of the crime and the accuser would give speeches presenting their sides of the story. The person with the best forensic skills usually won the case.

In the modern world, "forensics" has come to mean the various procedures, many of them scientific in nature, used to answer questions of interest to the legal system—usually, to solve a crime. Detective Kwan and the new members of the CSC will use many of these procedures in their cases. In this case, their eighth, the procedures involved with footprint analysis will prove to be particularly useful to them.

Forensic Procedures Used in CSC Case #8

DNA Analysis

Deoxyribonucleic acid, DNA for short, is the genetic code within the cells of a living organism that guides the development and function of an organism's life. Human DNA is composed of about 3 billion bases, about 99 percent of which are the same in all people. In 1985, an English geneticist named Dr. Alec Jeffreys discovered that certain regions of these bases were composed of sequences repeated multiple times right next to each other. The length of these repeat regions (called variable number of tandem repeats or VNTRs) varies from indi-

1.1 This 2007 photograph shows a Centers for Disease Control and Prevention biologist, preparing a "mastermix" for a PCR assay. Using PCR, very small amounts of nucleic acid molecules can be analyzed upon the completion of the replication process.

vidual to individual. By studying the length of the VNTRs it is possible to perform identity tests with DNA. The technique used to study the VNTRs is known as restriction fragment length polymorphism (RFLP) because a chemical called a restriction enzyme is used to cut the pieces of DNA surrounding the VNTRs.

Since the development of RFLP, the use of DNA analysis has become widespread as part of crime scene investigations. However, RFLP requires a large sample of DNA in order to complete the analysis accurately. Dr. Kary Mullis solved this problem with the development of the polymerase chain reaction (PCR), which takes a tiny fragment of DNA and copies it many times in a test tube. Using PCR, within a couple of hours a few DNA molecules can become a billion molecules. The invention of PCR allowed other DNA analysis techniques to gain importance in crime scene investigation. Short tandem repeat (STR) analysis is the most widely used method today because STRs are shorter in length and degradation is not as much of a concern as it is for the longer VNTRs needed in RFLP analysis. STRs are repeats of three to seven base pairs found commonly throughout an individual's DNA. Each place (locus) where the repeats occur only has a few variations between all individuals, but comparing several at once gives a DNA signature. In the United States, the FBI has selected thirteen specific loci as the standard for this signature. This standard of thirteen loci is stored in the FBI's Combined DNA Indexing System (CODIS), which is a database that the FBI uses to share and compare DNA signature results.

Fingerprinting

On the surfaces of the hands and feet are tiny raised wrinkles called friction ridges. These ridges are formed while a fetus is still developing within the uterus. Each person's friction ridges are unique; even identical twins do not have the same fingerprints. What's more, barring scarring or injury, friction ridges remain unchanged throughout life.

When friction ridges come in contact with a surface that is receptive to a print, any material on the ridges—such as perspiration, body oils, ink, or grease—can be transferred to the surface. As you move through life, your fingers (and toes, if you're barefoot) leave telltale marks behind.

1.2 A forensic latent print examiner inspects a soda can in search of fingerprints. The specialized lighting helps the hidden prints show up more clearly.

Chapter 2

Evidence List

Vocab Words

aghast
radical
activists
minimal

Deciphering the Evidence

Jessa was originally *aghast* at Sara Crown's suggestion of writing to a criminal, but she recovered from her initial shock and fear after discovering a fellow artist in prisoner Lewis Henry.

Lewis Henry was part a *radical* Native group that opposed the Diamondback Uranium mine; because his group used extreme actions to challenge the situation, an FBI agent ended up killed and Henry wound up in prison.

Who Are the Diné?

The Diné are the members of the Navajo Nation. *Diné* means "the people" in the Navajo language, and is the term that members traditionally use for themselves.

Lewis Henry and his group were *activists*, people who used direct action to oppose the Diamondback Mining Corporation.

Lewis calls prison medical care *minimal* at best, meaning the prison offers barely enough to be adequate.

What Do the Diné Believe?

The Diné are a very spiritual people, but do not have a word for religion. Rather the Diné strive for a state of balance and harmony (hózhó) by finding holiness in everyday life. Their creation story tells how the first people climbed through the lower worlds into this world and built the first Hogan (house); within this house they arranged their new world surrounded by four sacred mountains. The four mountains represent sacred materials (white shell, turquoise, abalone shell, and black jet) and mark north, south, east, and west. The Diné do not believe in one Supreme Being, but rather in several important supernatural beings: Changing Woman, the Hero Twins, Sun, First Man, First Woman, and the Diyinii (Holy People). Healing ceremonies, conducted by a hataali, bring the people into contact with these spirits, and help to restore health and harmony.

What Is Navajo Nation?

Navajo Nation (Diné Bikéyah) is the homeland of the Navajo, or Diné, people. The Nation covers over 27,000 square miles (approximately 69,231 square kilometers) and extends into the states of Arizona, New Mexico, and Utah. The Navajo Nation is the largest Indian Nation in North America, both in membership and landmass.

2.1 The traditional boundaries of Diné Bikéyah were the four sacred mountains that can be seen on this modern map of the Nation.

What Is Diabetes?

Diabetes is a disease in which blood sugar (glucose) levels are too high. Depending on the type of diabetes, the high glucose levels have different causes. Type 1 diabetes, also called juvenile onset diabetes, is a lifelong condition in which the body produces little or no insulin. Insulin is a hormone secreted by the pancreas gland just behind the stomach. Without enough insulin, glucose builds up in the bloodstream instead of entering cells.

More common than the juvenile-onset variety, Type 2 or adult-onset diabetes occurs when the body becomes resistant to the effects of insulin. Type 2 diabetes can occur in anyone, though the elderly, African Americans, Native Americans, Latinos, and Asian Americans have a higher risk of developing the disease, as do people who are overweight, especially those who have a high percentage of abdominal fat.

Symptoms of type 2 diabetes include fatigue, weight loss, extreme hunger, increased thirst, blurred vision, and frequent infections. If left untreated, diabetes can cause many serious complications, such as heart and blood vessel disease, nerve damage, kidney damage, and eye damage.

Type 2 diabetes can be effectively controlled with medication, but the best treatment is prevention. Leading a healthy lifestyle is one of the best ways to prevent this condition.

Chapter 3

Evidence List

Vocab Words

liability
allegedly
recidivism
requisition
transcripts

Deciphering the Evidence

Detective Kwan cannot assign another case
to the CSC because they are too much of a
liability. Dorothy will be responsible if the
club gets into trouble again, and she is not
willing to take that legal risk.

Lewis Henry is in prison for *allegedly* killing an FBI agent; he was found guilty, but
without hard evidence as proof that he
committed the murder.

Wire think *recidivism* rates are high because prisoners come out of jail with the
same DNA and hormones as before they
went in; they are bound to relapse and begin committing crimes again.

Detective Kwan likes Jessa's idea—she says
she will *requisition* all the original case materials. After she submits a formally writ-

ten request, Ms. Kwan expects the files will arrive by Monday.

Detective Kwan wants the CSC to go through all the original case files—*transcripts*, photographs, and anything else she can get. Perhaps the CSC will find a sentence in one of the official typewritten copies or a piece of hair from the original crime scene that will clear Lewis Henry's name.

Innocence Cases

An innocence case is any legal case or investigation in which a prisoner is seeking to clear his or her name of past wrongful convictions, in many cases by applying modern DNA evidence.

There are many reasons why a person might be wrongfully convicted. Race or ethnicity often seems to be a factor in cases like this. For example, Lewis Henry is a Native American who was tried and convicted by an all-white jury. Sometimes, police officers trick a suspect into confessing. In other cases, evidence is mishandled or disregarded. There are innocence cases in North America, and organizations such as the Innocence Network work to bring these cases to the public's attention through the database on their Web site. The network is a group of organizations that work to provide appropriate legal representation and investigative services to those individuals who are wrongfully convicted.

Chapter 4

Evidence List

Vocab Words

generated	incriminating
negligence	consistent
objective	trajectory
irrelevant	corrupted
strategic	opposing
caliber	traditional

Deciphering the Evidence

When Detective Kwan says that the Lewis Henry case *generated* a lot of public attention she means that the case created a lot of interest.

Diamondback Mining Corporation faced charges of *negligence*, but was successfully able to fight the claims of failure to protect its workers from harm.

Detective Kwan reminds the team students that it is important to remain *objective* about the case; they must review the facts without personal bias or prejudice.

When the CSC members begin arguing about the merits of being involved in a group like Act Now, Detective Kwan reminds them that their beliefs are *irrelevant*; they are unrelated to solving the case.

The shootout did not occur randomly, but as the result of a *strategic* attempt by the FBI and Diamondback Mining to unlock a chained gate. The activists were prepared for this carefully planned operation and fired shots to warn the agents away.

Frederick Allen was killed by two slugs from a .30-06 *caliber* gun, which means the bullet (or the barrel of the gun) has a diameter of about .30 in.

Lewis Henry and Dan Twogoats both carried *incriminating* weapons that matched the caliber of the murder weapon; this made them seem guilty.

The bullets the killed Agent Allen were *consistent* with Lewis Henry's gun, meaning marks on the bullets matched patterns expected for that type of gun.

McClintock's testimony of finding Lewis Henry standing behind Agent Allen's body is consistent with the bullet *trajectory*. The bullet traveled a path through the air behind the agent and entered the back of his head.

Though the ballistics expert weighed the slug to match up caliber, the rifling on the bullet was too *corrupted*, or ruined, to positively match the gun.

The original case came down to two *opposing* statements: Lewis Henry claiming he walked up to find the agent dead, and McClintock's conflicting story that he caught Henry with the smoking gun.

Jessa notices that a photograph from the crime scene depicts Lewis Henry in *traditional* moccasins, a style handed down from generation to generation.

Forensic Procedures Used in CSC Case #8

Ballistics and Firearms Identification

The study of movements and forces involved in the propulsion of objects through the air is known as ballistics. Ballistics can be applied to any object moving through

4.1 A forensic firearms examiner fires a rifle into a machine designed to catch the round to compare identifying marks on two rounds fired from the same rifle. Firearms evaluation of rounds helps determine if a weapon was used in a particular crime.

119

Uranium and Radiation

The element uranium (U), number 92 on the periodic table, is a silver-gray, dense metal that is weakly radioactive. Radioactive substances decay, or break down, and over time turn into other atoms. Natural uranium exists in ore deposits as a mixture of three different isotopes 238U (99.27%), 235U (0.72%), and 234U (0.0054%). The isotope most useful for nuclear technology is 235U. Uranium mining is the process of removing uranium ore from the ground, usually for the purpose of fueling nuclear power plants.

the air, but forensic ballistics is most commonly associated with bullets. A bullet has a high amount of energy when it leaves the barrel of a gun. As it travels, this energy decreases, until eventually the bullet drops to the ground. The factors in between the time the bullet was fired and when it hit the ground are what a forensic ballistics expert must take into account when trying to determine a shooter's location. How far did the bullet travel? What did it hit along the way?

A bullet trajectory can be determined by finding points of entry and exit and by drawing a straight line along the suspected path of travel. The case against Lewis Henry was in part built on his being found behind the body, a location consistent with the entry and exit wounds in the head.

Firearms identification involves studying bullets and bullet casings to determine the bullet manufacturer, the caliber, and the gun type. Different types of guns leave different markings on bullets and casings, depending on the rifling of the barrel of the gun. Rifling is the pattern of grooves that curve around the inside of a barrel of a gun. Firearms experts will shoot bullets from a suspected gun and then compare them to bullets from the crime scene to try and make a positive match. In this case, the expert was unable to make a match because the rifling marks on the bullets were too corrupted. In cases when the expert does not have a suspected weapon, marks from a bullet can be compared to marks that are held in nationwide computer databases.

Fast Fact

The worst nuclear disaster occurred on April 26, 1986 at the Chernobyl Nuclear Power Plant in the Ukraine. According to a 2005 report by the Chernobyl Forum, 56 deaths are directly attributed to the disaster, while up to 4,000 additional deaths may indirectly result.

Establishing a Motive

Determining who has a motive—a reason—to commit a crime helps detectives identify likely suspects. Motive alone is not proof, but when combined with "means" (the ability) and the "opportunity" to commit a crime, it can lead to a jury conviction. This is part of the reason that Lewis Henry is in prison. He had a known motive, an incriminating weapon, and was found standing behind the victim. Even without the hard evidence, it is not hard to see why the jury had no trouble finding him guilty.

A Native Perspective on Terrorism's Roots

Homeland Security—what does this phrase mean to you? Since just after September 11, 2001 it has been the title of the United States' government department in charge of preparing for and protecting the nation from threats to civilians, particularly the threat of terrorism. The T-shirt Maeve mentions— "Homeland Security: Fighting Terrorism Since 1492"—is a witty, but harsh reminder that when Europeans first arrived in the Americas they were more terrorist than protector. The native people already living here were attacked, enslaved, and killed—all while their homeland was being stolen out from under them.

Nuclear Power, Pros and Cons

Nuclear power uses energy created by nuclear reactions to generate electricity. Nuclear energy is released in the process called nuclear fission, during which atoms in a nucleus are split apart to form smaller atoms. Nuclear power plants can generate a lot of electricity, the technology is already available, and nuclear power is clean—emitting low levels of CO_2, and so contributing less to global warming than other forms of energy. These pros make nuclear energy seem an obvious energy choice; however, the cons of nuclear power also make a strong case. The first negative is the dangerous radioactive waste products, which have to be contained for thousands of years. Nuclear power may not be sustainable, because uranium is already a scarce resource. New power plants can take up to 30 years to build, so this may not be a fast solution to the energy crisis. Finally, there are the risks of another meltdown catastrophe, like those that occurred at Chernobyl or Three Mile Island.

The O.J. Simpson Case

In the mid-1990s, O.J. Simpson, a former football star and minor actor, was famously put on trial for the double murder of his ex-wife, Nicole Brown Simpson, and her friend Ronald Coleman. The case has become famous for many reasons, one of which is mentioned by Detective Kwan—the mistakes made by the police in collecting and preserving the vital material evidence. These mistakes led the defense to argue that the police had tampered with evidence, an argument that ultimately defeated the charges against Simpson.

The fact that police had made many mistakes in their collection of evidence allowed for what is called reasonable doubt, meaning that there was the possibility that Simpson was innocent. Despite their belief that Simpson committed the murders, jurors could not convict him because of this reasonable doubt.

Chapter 5

Evidence List

Vocab Words

venerable

consignment

Hogan

irregularities

prosecutors

falsified

animated

liberal

Deciphering the Evidence

Despite his *venerable* years, Stanley Peshlaki seems young, not old.

Stanley Peshlaki sells his artwork on *consignment* at the Snow Owl Gallery, an arrangement where they pay him only for what he sells.

Mr. Peshlaki invites Jessa to his *Hogan*, his traditional Diné home made of logs and dirt, having 6 or 8 sides.

When Jessa tells Ken the have turned up an *irregularity* in the case files, she means that they have found a place where the evidence does not match up smoothly.

If the *prosecutors*, the lawyers presenting the case against the defendant Lewis Henry, switched evidence, then it seems like they were deliberately trying to frame him.

Jessa is suggesting that the investigators *falsified* evidence, and presented information and materials that weren't the truth.

In her excitement over the case, Jessa grows more *animated*—forgetting her discomfort, she moves more and is livelier.

Ella Allen complains that *liberal*-minded people have tried to free Lewis Henry before; she thinks these individuals are too broad-minded and tolerant of Henry's actions.

What Is Sand Painting?

Sand painting, also called dry painting, uses tiny grains of sand and other natural substances to create an image. The pictures are created and then destroyed on the floor of a Hogan as part of Diné ceremonies.

What Is the Beauty Way?

The Beauty way is another way of referring to the Diné concept of Hozho, or harmony. Walking the beauty way refers not to walking as in the physical movement, but the "walking" of your spirit through the world in harmony with all people, all the animals, all the supernatural beings, and all the objects around you. It is a concept of being at total peace with everything in the surrounding world.

Chain of Custody

The chain of custody of evidence is the record of every person who has come into contact with that evidence. In a criminal case, the fewer people who handle the evidence the better, but if evidence must be handled there are particular protocols that must be followed to preserve any trace evidence, fingerprints, or DNA evidence that may be present.

In maintaining the chain of custody it is also vital to keep a clear written record of exactly where and when individuals did come into contact with the evidence. After all, on a crime scene investigation, if an agent finds a piece of evidence, someone will have to pick it up eventually. The evidence needs to be packed and transported for secure storage or additional testing in a laboratory. Labels include information such as the name/initials of the individual collecting the evidence; each person who subsequently touched the evidence; dates the items were collected and then transferred from person to person; from where the item(s) were collected; agency and case number; victim's or suspect's name; and a brief description of the item.

Chapter 6

Evidence List

Vocab Words

antagonistic
plausible
implicating
candor

Deciphering the Evidence

When Jessa and Detective Kwan first arrive at Mrs. McClintock's home, she does not seem to be *antagonistic*, or hostile, toward them.

Bob McClintock's explanation for his raise was *plausible* at first, but now Mrs. McClintock finds it less believable.

Detective Kwan warns Mrs. McClintock that the rifle and boots could be evidence *implicating* her husband—connecting him to—some dishonesty.

Mrs. McClintock's openness and honesty could be of great help to the case; her *candor* might even free Lewis Henry.

Footprint Forensics

Footprints (from bare feet) are as individual as fingerprints. Like fingers, toes have a pattern of ridges and release sweat and oils that leave behind residues when the foot touches a surface. The FBI actually maintains a database of big toe prints, especially for individuals who have no fingerprints.

Another aspect of footprint forensics is barefoot morphology, which is the study of the prints left by the weight-bearing portions of the foot, rather than the ridges. Barefoot impressions may be retrieved from mud, blood, or other soft substances. Barefoot morphology can also be used to match a suspect's feet to a particular pair of shoes based on the indentations created on the inside of the shoes.

Shoe print evidence is less unique than footprint evidence, because more than one person can wear the same size and even buy the same style and brand of shoe. However, over time, shoes acquire unique wear patterns on the soles (and on the inside). The soles of shoes also collect debris, such as blood, hair, or dirt that might tie a suspect to the crime scene.

As with fingerprints, shoe prints can be latent (invisible) or visible. A print that is clearly visible can be cast with plaster or another casting material. The cast preserves the print, but it is only the impression made by the shoe. In order to see what the shoe itself looked like, a negative image cast must be made. Hidden latent prints can be made visible through dusting, or by spraying with a chemical agent.

Chapter 7

Evidence List

Vocab Words

transformed   symbolic
expertise   controversial
customary   acquittal
perception

Deciphering the Evidence

When working with technology, Wire is *transformed*, he is changed.

The Lewis Henry case will need the skill and knowledge of an excellent team of lawyers, and that kind of legal *expertise* is expensive.

Wire's *customary* way of speaking is in monotone; only when excited about a computer project does he break out of his usual habit.

Public *perception* will be very important in Lewis Henry's innocence case. The CSC will need to campaign to ensure the public understanding and thoughts about the case are the same as theirs.

Jessa is ready to paint *symbolic* pieces for an exhibition; the paintings will use other images to stand for the Lewis Henry case.

Detective Kwan is not sure about the *controversial* exhibition plan, because she is afraid it will a source of argument.

Acquittal for Lewis Henry, or the clearing of his name, will come at the cost of a conviction for Bob McClintock.

Who Was Machiavelli?

Niccolò Machiavelli, usually referred to as Machiavelli, was a politician and philosopher of Florence during the fifteenth and sixteenth centuries. Machiavelli is best remembered for a book published after he died. Machiavelli's *The Prince* was written as a guide for a ruler to keep control of his city. The book recommends the use of any means necessary to gain the desired ends. The book's focus on success, even if it requires sacrificing one's morals, earned Machiavelli a reputation so that today the word Machiavellian means ruthless or without morals.

Forensic Procedures Used in CSC Case #8

Forensic Photography

Photography is used to document many types of evidence, including foot print and shoe print evidence. At a crime scene, the forensic photographers capture the scene before anything is touched. The photographs can be used to simply record the surrounding conditions and evidence at the time of the crime—but they can also be taken back to the lab, where computers are used to enhance details on the photographs that might not otherwise be discernable to the human eye.

Recent advances in digital imaging have greatly improved many aspects of forensic photography. Digital techniques allow detectives and the lab technicians who help them to capture, edit, output, and transfer images faster than they could with processed film. In the old days, when photographers de-

7.1 This forensic science consultant carefully pours a dental solution into a footprint to

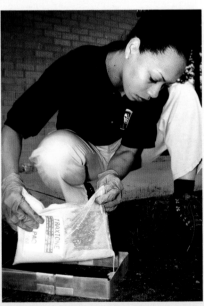

get a three-dimensional cast of the shoe sole. Casting results in a hardened mold in about 45 minutes. It can also be used to take car tire impressions as well as two-dimensional impressions of footprints on slick floor surfaces or fingerprints on windowsills.

pended on darkrooms, many techniques had to be applied through time-consuming trial and error; now, with digital photography, these techniques can be instantly applied on a computer, and the results are immediately visible on the monitor.

More Firearms

Firearms experts use a tank filled with water to fire bullets into during rifling tests. The water causes less damage to the bullets than other substances and leaves enough of the bullet intact for comparisons to be made. Water does damage the bullets as they break the surface tension, however, and firearms companies are working to develop new technologies that will cause even less damage to

What Is Diabetic Shock?

Diabetic shock, or hypoglycemia, happens when there is too little glucose available in the bloodstream (low blood sugar). Hypoglycemia is most common in people being treated for diabetes. The low blood sugar can cause heart palpitations, sweating, anxiety, tremors, and extreme hunger. If levels go too low, the brain has trouble functioning normally. This can result in confusion, blurred vision, seizures and even loss of consciousness.

bullets and allow for improvements in the
bullet identification process.

Public Perception and Justice

Sometimes the public's opinion of a case, or
of a defendant, may change the verdict. If
the public perception of a defendant is that
he is guilty, prosecutors may seek harsher
charges and sentences. Juries might become
biased, and because of this, steps are taken
to isolate jurors during high-profile cases,
so that their decision will be objective. Even
judges might be swayed by a large group of
people who think a certain way about the
case. These human biases are always present in criminal cases—the court system is
run by people, after all—but there are ways
of preventing cases from being entirely al-
tered by perception.

Established in 1992 by Barry C. Scheck
and Peter J. Neufeld, the Innocence Project
is committed to freeing those criminals who
can be proven innocent with DNA evidence
that might not have been able to be used in
the past. While Lewis Henry's case does not
deal with DNA evidence, the CSC's idea of
raising public awareness of his case is quite
similar to the mission of the Innocence
Project. Public perception has a powerful
potential to change the outcome of cases,
but not every case gets the same amount of
media and public attention. Groups like the
Innocence Project attempt to raise awareness of lower profile cases in order to free
those who deserve to be free.

Chapter 8

Evidence List

Vocab Words

left-wing
conclusive
inscrutable
DA

Deciphering the Evidence

Some people thought only *left-wing* crazies wanted to free Lewis Henry, but the art exhibition proves it is not just a radical idea.

Mrs. Allen agrees that the evidence looks *conclusive*; she believes that it is putting an end the debate about Henry's innocence.

Detective Kwan has an *inscrutable* look, an unreadable expression, on her face.

The *district attorney* (*DA*), the local public official that represents the government in trials against alleged criminals, has granted Lewis Henry a retrial.

Footprint Forensics

Here's something you can do to better understand how detectives use footprints to track down criminals.

Have some adults remove their shoes and measure their height.
Measure the length of the adult's left foot from the wall to the tip of the big toe. Examine the numbers. Do you see a pattern?

Divide the length of each person's left foot by his or her height. Multiply the quotient by 100. What do you get? The results of your calculations should be about 15, showing that the length of a person's foot is approximately 15 percent of his or her height.

See if you can determine the approximate height of each of your classmates by measuring his or her foot and charting it on a spreadsheet. Use this proportion for your calculations:

$$15/100 = \text{Length of Foot}/x \text{ (person's height)}$$

When a forensic scientist has the length of a foot, she will be able to approximate the height of the individual. This works best on a full-grown individual, since the ratio of body parts is slightly different in growing children.

Chapter 9

Evidence List

Vocab Words

repercussions
harassing
chagrined
recoiled

Deciphering the Evidence

Diamondback Mining Corporation doesn't think there will be any *repercussions* for reopening the Lewis Henry case. There will be no new effects because of the events of the past.

Jessa hopes that the Diamondback Corporation will stop *harassing* the CSC. She hates that they are only helping Henry for selfish reasons, but will be happy if they stop bothering her and her friends.

Ken looked *chagrined* when Jessa put him down, because he is truly upset with himself over the situation.

Jessa pulled back from touching Ken's ring; she *recoiled* because she is not ready to take that step yet.

Wrapping Up CSC Case #8

Truth is the major theme of Case # 8. Jessa struggles with accepting the truths in her life: her mother's boyfriend abused Jessa and her mother didn't seem to care; Ken cheated on her; and one of her best friends was killed by her husband. Even while struggling to accept her own problems, she is a part of the Crime Scene Club, a group that is dedicated to seeking the truth, no matter how confusing. After all, the truth may set people free, but it also locks some people up.

In the case, Jessa repeatedly finds out how truly complicated the truth can get. While working on the case, she is approached by the widow of the murdered FBI agent, who begs her to drop the case; the CSC successfully set Lewis Henry free, only to find out after that he was guilty of abusing his daughter; Jessa confronts her mother about her own past abuses and realizes that her mother was as trapped as she was.

In the end, Jessa realizes that living for the truth and being honest with oneself may not always be the easy road, but it is the best way to walk through the world in beauty.

FURTHER READING

Bodziak, W, J., Forensic Footwear Evidence. *Forensic Science: An Introductory Guide*. Boca Raton, FL: CRC Press, 2003.

Campbell, Andrea. *Forensic Science: Evidence, Clues, and Investigation*. Philadelphia, PA: Chelsea House Publishers, 2000.

Craig, Emily. *Teasing Secrets from the Dead. My Investigations at America's Most Infamous Crime Scenes*. New York, NY: Crown Publishers, 2004.

Evans , Colin. *The Casebook of Forensic Detection: How Science Solved 100 of the World's Most Baffling Crimes*. New York: John Wiley & Sons, 1996.

Ferllini, Roxana. *Silent Witness. How Forensic Anthropology is Used to Solve the World's Toughest Crimes*. Buffalo, NY: Firefly Books, 2002.

Innes, Brian. *Forensic Science*. Philadelphia, PA: Mason Crest Publishers, 2006.

Morton, James. *Catching the Killers: A History of Crime Detection*. London, England: Ebury Press, 2001.

FOR MORE INFORMATION

All About Forensic Science. "Forensic Footwear Evidence."
http://www.forensic-courses.com/wordpress/?s=footwear+Footwear & Tire Track Impression Evidence. http://members.aol.com/varfee/mastssite/index.html

Crime and Clues, http://www.crimeandclues.com/

Crime Library, "Forensic Files,"
http://www.trutv.com/shows/forensic_files/techniques/print.html

Forensic Impression Footwear Analysis,
http://www.everything2.com/e2node/Forensic%2520footwear%2520impression%2520analysis

How Stuff Works, "How Crime Scene Investigation Works," www.howstuffworks.com/csi.htm

BIBLIOGRAPHY

Bodziak, William J. *Footwear Impression Evidence: Detection, Recovery and Examination.* Boca Raton, FL: CRC Press, 1999.

Genge, N. E. 2002. *The Forensic Casebook.* New York: Ballantine Books.

Lyle, D.P. 2004. *Forensics for Dummies.* Indianapolis, IN: Wiley Publishing Inc.

Naples, Virginia L. and Jon S. Mille. "Making tracks: The forensic analysis of footprints and footwear impressions." *The Anatomical Record.* Vol 279B(1), 2006.

Owen, David. 2000. *Hidden Evidence. Forty True Crimes and How Forensic Science Helped Solved Them.* Buffalo, NY: Firefly Books

Wecht, Cyril H. 2004. *Crime Scene Investigation.* Pleasantville, NY: The Reader's Digest Association, Inc.

INDEX

ballistics 119–121
beauty way 126

chain of custody 127
CODIS 109–110

diabetes 114
    diabetic shock 133
Dine 111, 112, 113
DNA 108–110
    analysis 108–110
    CODIS 109–110
    evidence 134
    PCR 109
    RLFP 109
    signature 108–110
    VNTR 108–109

fingerprinting 109
firearms 119–121, 133
    water tank 133
footprint analysis 107,
128–129, 135–136
    barefoot morphology
        129
    latent 129
    shoeprint 129
    visible 129
forensics
    definition 107
    footprints 128–129,
        135–136

history 107
photography 131–133

innocence cases 116, 134

justice
    and public perception
        134

Machiavelli 131
motive 121–122

Navajo 111, 112, 113
    Nation 113
nuclear power 123

PCR 109
photography 131–133
    computers 132
    digital 132–133

Queen Victoria 107

RFLP 109

sand painting 126
Sherlock Holmes 106
Simpson, O.J. 124

terrorism 122

VNTR 108–109

PICTURE CREDITS

Centers for Disease Control and Prevention
    Gathany, James: p. 108

United States Air Force
    Jones, Bobby: p. 132

United States Army
    Kent, Sgt. Jess: p. 110, 119

To the best knowledge of the publisher, all images not specifically credited are in the public domain. If any image has been inadvertently uncredited, please notify Harding House Publishing Service, Vestal, New York 13850, so that credit can be given in future printings.

BIOGRAPHIES

Author

Kenneth McIntosh is a freelance writer and college instructor who lives in beautiful Flagstaff, Arizona (while CSC is fictional, Flagstaff is definitely real). He has enjoyed crime fiction—from Sherlock Holmes to CSI and Bones—and is thankful for the opportunity to create his own detective stories. Now, if he could only find his car keys . . .

Ken would like to thank the following people:

Tom Oliver, who invented the title 'Crime Scene Club' on a tram en route to the Getty Museum, and cooked up the best plots while we sat at his Tiki bar . . . Mr. Levin's Creative Writing students at the Flagstaff Arts and Leadership Academy, *who vetted the books . . . Rob and Jenny Mullen and Victor Viera, my Writer's Group, who shared their lives and invaluable insights . . . My recently deceased father, Dr. A Vern McIntosh, who taught me when I was a child to love written words. This series could not have happened without all of you.*

Series Consultant

Carla Miller Noziglia is Senior Forensic Advisor, Tanzania, East Africa, for the U.S. Department of Justice, International Criminal Investigative Training Assistant Program. A Fellow of the American Academy of Forensic Sciences her work has earned her many honors and commendations, including Distinguished Fellow from the American Academy of Forensic Sciences (2003) and the Paul L. Kirk Award from the American Academy of Forensic Sciences Criminalistics Section. Ms. Noziglia's publications include *The Real Crime Lab* (coeditor, 2005), *So You Want to be a Forensic Scientist* (coeditor 2003), and contributions to *Drug Facilitated Sexual Assault* (2001), *Convicted by Juries, Exonerated by Science: Case Studies in the Use of DNA* (1996), and the *Journal of Police Science* (1989).

Illustrator

Justin Miller first discovered art while growing up in Gorham, ME. He developed an interest in the intersection between science and art at the University of New Hampshire while studying studio art and archaeology. He applies both degrees in his job at the Public Archaeology Facility at Binghamton University. He also enjoys playing soccer, hiking, and following English Premier League football.